You're everything to me

Beauty in the field, sun on my skin
Cool of the night, taste on my lips

In battle and storm, peace in the wind
My rock when You're near, strength past my end

Love reaching from everlasting to everlasting
You're everything to me

MORE THAN CONQUERORS

ON THE RUN

DJANÉE

Second Edition, 2025
Dreams & Visions Publishing
Dallas, TX
(972) 855-8543
www.djaneecreations.com

Cover Design: MiblArt
Editing & Proofreading: Leonora Stewart, Alexandra Ott
Library of Congress Control Number: 2024920197
ISBN: 979-8-9885063-7-9 (paperback)
ISBN: 979-8-9993938-0-7 (paperback)
ISBN: 979-8-9885063-9-3 (ebook)

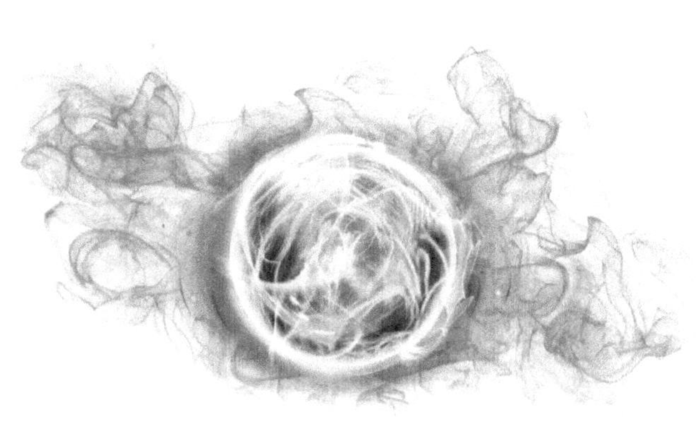

MORE THAN CONQUERORS

ON THE RUN

DJANÉE

Table of Contents

Chapter 1

I AM RUNNING, AND I am searching. The three of us have split up to look for a way out. As soon as someone locates an exit, we will *signal* the others there. We should be all right separated. We might be young, but we can defend ourselves.

I trudge through a homogeneous system of long, endless tunnels, every turn putting me in a new stretch that is the same as the last. The long, bland gray hallways truly make me feel like I am in a prison. Where am I? Where are we? I have no idea, but I do know this: We are not going to stay here. We are going to succeed. We are going to escape ... somehow.

Time passes as I aimlessly run through this labyrinth, which means that none of us has found a way out yet. We are mice scurrying through infinite, captivating tunnels, after the cheese of a Prophecy of freedom and safety. I have to wonder if the Envisionment was wrong, but I cast that thought aside. Prophecies are never wrong. There has to be a way out.

If only I could burrow or simply walk through these walls. But I do not have such a *gift* that could so easily help me find something—anything—that would get me out of here. My only option is my *force field*, which is not much help, because I am not well-trained in using it yet. Nevertheless, I stop running a few times and extend my *force field* down several corridors, feeling for a way out—anything other than this depressing, hopeless maze—but I find nothing. I have to keep moving. I do not know what lurks in these narrow hallways, nor do I want to run into undesirable company.

Infinite time passes, and I am growing weary. My muscles are exhausted. Sweat makes the dark gray suit I was given stick to my body, and my breathing is loud from the endless running. My feet pound against the floor, mixing with my shallow breaths in echoes that reverberate throughout the narrow corridors around me, and my body is too fatigued to minimize the ruckus. I cringe internally with every echo that bounces back to my ears, but I cannot stop. There is no time. Every moment spent recovering my breath could mean that one of my friends runs into trouble. At any moment, it may be discovered that we are missing from our cell. Then, they will come after us again ... the Firebursts.

I do not know what strikes me with fear the most: the threat of being caught—though I know that the Prophecy said we would escape—or the possibility of wandering through these tormenting gray halls for eternity. In the case of the latter, what would happen to us? Starvation? Eventually, we would wind up with the first threat that plagues me. One of us would be caught.

Then what would they do to us? Torture us? They only need one of us. They would stir up enough pain or rage to unintentionally *signal* the others to their side, back into captivity. We are only skilled enough to tug or inform others as to our location by *signaling* them. But if there is enough turmoil to provoke our energy, I am sure that one of us could fully teleport the others right back into captivity. No, I have to keep moving. And yes, we are going to get out of here.

I am approaching the end of a long corridor, where another stretches to the left and right. I feel little hope of finding anything useful down either side, but I keep pushing my legs forward, ignoring the burn in my muscles.

As I approach the intersection, a person in a bundle of orange comes into view beyond the corner, sitting against the wall and hugging their knees. I freeze in my tracks as I realize that it is a frightened child … and they are not alone. In baggy orange suits, several children sit against the wall, side by side with wide eyes and trembling with fear. A bigger bundle of orange, with disheveled jet-black hair cascading over her shoulders, sits at the far end of the line. She hugs her knees as well, and her head is tucked in her arms. She is probably an adult. There is something unidentifiably peculiar about the woman, but I dismiss it.

I am confused. The Envisionment did not depict anything about helpless people. Then again, it did not mention anything about perturbing alleyways of swarming gray either. Regardless, I cannot leave them here.

I rush to the aid of the frightened children nearest me. As soon as they see me approaching, they recoil in terror, curling into one another and cringing against the wall as though they could push it back to get away from me. It must be because of our different suits. Unlike their baggy orange ones, I am wearing a fitted, dark gray suit with subtle designs of dark crescents. They must think that I am a Fireburst.

"No, no, no," I urge, trying to soothe them. "I am not going to hurt you." I look deep into their eyes, trying to reassure them that they can trust me. If they are captives here like I am, I can certainly understand their terror. These Firebursts are ruthless and cruel, and I have the marks to prove it.

Nonetheless, their fear is dangerous. Their emotional hysteria could stimulate an outburst of power, rendering a terminal threat both to them and to me. And I dare not speculate what kinds of *gifts* they have. I need to calm them down. Now.

"Shh, shh, shh, shh, shh. Do not cry."

I am about to rest my hand on a child's knee when the row of orange bundles begins to change. The children start to ... *merge.* They combine in a blurry, vibrating vision. Whatever powerful *gift* this is, these children are actually a single individual. For a person to not simply *clone* themselves but divide into distinctive persons is astonishing.

My attention is drawn back to the woman at the end of the line as the children sequentially *merge* into each other, one after another, toward her. She slowly raises her head, and my heart leaps in my chest with fear as I realize what is so peculiar about her.

Fear is never good, but there are far more pressing matters at hand. I should have kept running. I should have seen the red skin of her hands and of her neck peeking out from under the orange suit—a far deeper red than the sunburnt color of Firebursts. I was too preoccupied with what I thought were innocent children to take notice of her. What alarms me now is her red face, which is covered with what look like acne scars, welts, and the marks of someone who has been burned with fire.

I am facing a Killer, and her obvious target is me. The Firebursts have sent an assassin to kill us. They know that we have escaped, which means that Josh and Jules are in danger too and that I am already dead.

My heart hammers in my chest when she flashes a mischievous, knowing grin at me, and I know that she will enjoy killing me. But ... the Prophecy. She cannot kill me—

Poof!

Poof!

I am called out and back into existence in a large, peculiar white room filled with rows of empty shelving units. I stand in one of the aisles. A tall unit is to my left and a short one to my right, but there are no people here. This place is foreign and distant from where I was, but I cannot dwell on that, because my body panics at the sight of the Killer standing a few feet in front of me, preparing to execute her assignment.

I know what the Prophecy said, but a terrifying pledge of death stands before me. And though I am unfamiliar with Killers, I have heard the rumors of their great power back at home—before it was destroyed.

Memories of fire and chaos, wreaked by the Firebursts that ran rampant through our home, flash through my mind before the anxiety clutching my heart brings me back to the present. They stimulate a heightened sense of vigilance as my energy courses through my veins. I may be afraid, but my focus is sharpened, and time slows so that I do not miss a single moment. Emotional stimuli can be powerful weapons. I just need to use them to my advantage. Josh, Jules, and I are the only survivors from the attack, and we barely made it out. It cannot be for nothing.

I study my opponent as I ready myself for battle. Her dark eyes practically blaze with flames, and her red skin forewarns of her dangerous power as she observes me with intense focus. I am just another disposable target to her, but I do not let this overwhelm me. I brace myself.

With a subtle smirk, she crouches and then lunges into the air, hands outstretched with the anticipation of ending my life. I ignore the distraction of her intimidating eagerness and swiftly throw my hands up, projecting a *force field* around her until I can feel her whole body engulfed in it. I hold her in my *field*, suspended in midair, only a couple of feet from my face.

Suddenly constrained, the aerial Killer's menacing smile

transforms into an expression of shock. Despite the panic that still travels through my veins, I am tempted to return a sly sneer of mockery to her, but I choose not to. I stay focused, because just a single distraction could make me lose control of my *field*.

My body immediately fatigues under her weight. Already my arms tremble from the strain, and I cannot suspend her much longer. I swing my hands down to the right, releasing my *field* to throw her into the short shelving unit. It topples into the next aisle as the assassin crashes into it. Before she can recover, my hands catch her in my *field* again. I pull her back into the air, only to yank her to the floor, but my heart skips into my throat when she passes right through it.

I have underestimated Killers. The rumors at home of their vast capabilities were all too accurate, which means that I am in even more danger than I thought. Now this Killer is lurking somewhere with practically limitless power, preparing to attack and kill me, and I have no idea where.

I am frantic. I swing my head wildly back and forth, desperately seeking her. I look for any sign of red skin or jet-black hair, but I find none. Standing in one place makes me feel too vulnerable and stiff. If she suddenly jumps out from somewhere, I will probably be too paralyzed with fear to move. I need to stay fluid so that I can defend myself when the time comes.

I slowly advance with quiet, deliberate steps. Everything is silent, with the exception of my heartbeat pounding in my ears and the soft, shaky breaths that stagger from my lips. I close my mouth to silence myself. I do not want to give away my position. For all I know, the Killer may have some *gift* of *sensitive hearing* too. Besides, I need to hear her if she is near me.

My breathing is still harsh and jagged through my nose, but it is quieter. I need to ignore all fear, and I need to focus. My eyes and ears are on high alert as I search for my pursuer.

I reach an intersection. More rows of white shelving units extend along my left and right. I proceed down the same aisle and take every step cautiously, expecting the Killer to suddenly lunge at any moment.

I am trapped in yet another maze, endlessly wondering what lurks just outside my peripheral vision and when I will finally be free from captivity, when I think of my friends. Perhaps they have escaped. Maybe they are trying to *signal* me to join them, and I simply have not felt it yet. Perhaps I am too far away from them, or too frightened, to feel their tug without conscientiously searching for it within myself. Perhaps they are free and safe, and I can be too.

Hope erupts inside me, and I think that maybe—just

maybe—I do not have to face this assassin. Maybe I can leave and wake up from this horrifying, cyclical nightmare. If I am too distracted by fear to detect their *signal*, then I need to quell my emotions and concentrate in order to find it. I need to make myself feel safer somehow. My only option is my *force field*.

My energy is still depleted. But feeding on the hope of escape, I am about to surround myself with my *field* when black hair appears over the low shelving unit on my right, sending my hopes crashing down in a heap of massacred expectations.

Perhaps I can contend with her, delaying the end, but I cannot imagine how that end will include my victory and her demise. The Prophecy flashes across my mind, and I do not know what to believe as she elevates from the floor in my direction, searching for me. I choose to cling to the Prophecy, because there is too much to live for. Perhaps, somehow, I can get through this.

She is right beside me when our eyes meet, and she lunges over the low shelving unit. I jerk my hands up to catch her in my *field* again, and she is frozen with a look of rage. She must have expected that she was close enough to catch me off-guard before I could defend myself.

She no longer wears the arrogant smirk that she wore earlier nor the loose orange fabric I found her in. She now wears a fitted black suit similar to mine.

My thoughts are interrupted by the protest in my arms against her weight again. I swiftly slam her into the taller shelves on my left, knocking the wind out of her as they topple under her into the neighboring aisle. As they crash, I throw my *field* around her again and toss her into the low shelves on my right with fatigued arms.

She grunts as the blow knocks the wind out of her lungs again, and I am encouraged by my success. I do not know exactly what injuries I am inflicting, but it is evident that I am accomplishing some level of effective combat. I cannot keep this up forever, though. My only hope is to leave with Josh and Jules, and I think that I feel something from them.

Hope ignites in me again. I need to get into a safer position, and I need time. I need to get rid of this Killer somehow.

The Killer tries to get up, but I do not let her arms budge before I grab her with my *field* again. I pull her back into the center of the aisle and thrust my hands down as forcefully as I can, the Killer disappearing through the floor again with a smirk just before going through, perhaps thinking that she will return for me. But what she does not know is that I will not be here.

I waste no time. I do not even check my surroundings for

threats. I could not fight her anymore if I tried. I throw my *field* around myself and close my eyes to focus, relaxing my body in the moment of relative safety.

The pull is more noticeable, and it quickly intensifies as my body unwinds. It spreads from deep within to my extremities, extending to my arms, my hands, my legs, my feet—to every molecule of my body simultaneously. I can sense that it is Josh. Behind my closed eyelids, I can see him sitting somewhere in the dark and a hazy vision of his environment: a large window illuminates a long dining table, a few big books sit in a far corner, and a large chandelier looks exceptionally old and ornate. I can feel Josh's tranquility. He is calm. He is safe. And in a moment, I will be too.

Relief floods my entire body, but I realize that I do not sense Jules. I do not feel her, and I do not see her. Where is she?

I surrender to Josh's *signal*, entering some element of peace. I open my eyes, content with my travel arrangements, but am alarmed by a red face soaring through the air at my own with burns, scars, and a terrifying scowl of rage framed by black hair and clawed hands.

Poof!

Poof!

I stand still, recovering from the shock. She could not have hurt me with my *field* up, but one hard collision could have depleted my residual strength so that I could not defend myself against anything else. I am not sure that I would have even had enough strength to follow Josh's *signal* to safety.

I wipe the thoughts from my mind. Whatever could have happened did not. I am safe now—wherever I am.

It takes a while for my eyes to adjust to the dim lighting after coming from the bright white space. I blink a few times as the mysterious dark objects surrounding me develop details and character. As everything comes into focus, I realize that this is the mansion that the Prophecy revealed to us earlier today in the prison. The Envisionment in the crystal ball showed us this very place.

The room that I am standing in is quite empty, but large and spacious, with occasional cobwebs and a light layer of dust. It gives off an extravagant presence that seems ancient but endearing. Judging by the appearance of the mansion, evidently no one has lived here for a very long time. I have never seen an establishment like this before.

The maroon ceiling towers above me, and the maroon walls extend far from me. I spot the pile of books that I saw while being *signaled*. It lies on the floor in the corner of a protrusion in the wall that features a black door with elaborate carvings in it. I suppose it opens to an oddly positioned closet. To the left is an open door leading to a hallway with a brown banister connecting two staircases: one ascending to a higher level and one descending below.

I turn to my left to investigate and find the tall window and long dining table. The window looks down from its high place in the wall and pours in a faint twilight glow of orange and yellow, which spotlights the fine dust particles in the air and sprawls across the table. Ten tall, flamboyant chairs stand around the table: four lining either side and one at each end. That is only on one side of the room, by the wall. The rest of the massive space is vacant, with nothing more to show for itself than the creaky wooden floor, the maroon walls, and the grandiose chandelier that hangs from the ceiling with candle arms and trailing ornaments of pearls and crystals.

There is something in my peripheral vision on the floor in front of me.

"Sophie," Josh says.

I look down and see him peering up at me. The faint glow from the window behind him softly illuminates his brown hair but does not reach his face, except for a smudge of light that touches part of his forehead. It is probably a reflection from the chandelier. As he gets up, the light crosses his face and is gone.

"You made it."

The light behind his silhouette clearly defines his frame. He barely exceeds my height by an inch or two. I still cannot see his face, but knowing that he is next to me—simply hearing his voice and seeing his silhouette—makes me feel at rest. He is familiar. We no longer have a home, and we are on the run. This is as close to home as it gets for me right now, and it is strongly welcome after what I have just gone through.

"Yes." I nod. "I made it." I say it more to myself than to him. I feel relieved to say it. It is good to know that I am safe—that my encounter with the Killer is in the past. The battle is over. And as it turns out, I survived it after all.

I still do not see Jules. She must be in a different room. I open my mouth to ask about her, but Josh speaks first.

"Where have you been? I have been trying to *signal* you here for a while now." There is a reprimanding tone of urgency in his voice, and I can tell that he was worried. Apparently, I could have fled to safety a while ago, but I was too preoccupied to even notice Josh's attempt to get my attention. My mind flashes back to the haunting red face and the outstretched claws that were coming for me. Josh has no idea what I just went through.

"I ... ran into some trouble."

A beat of silence passes between us.

His voice softens when he asks, "What kind of trouble?"

I freeze. I may be safe, but I do not want to talk about it so soon. It is one thing to think about it, but it feels far worse to speak about it out loud. I do not want to mention anything about the Killer, but I tell myself that the encounter no longer matters because it is in the past. There is no reason to be afraid of her anymore.

I inhale deeply and then let it out. "A Killer."

I cannot see Josh's expression, but judging by his silence, I know that he is stunned—or maybe he is trying to decipher if I am making an unsuitable joke.

He crosses his arms and puts a fist under his chin. "A Killer?" I cannot tell if he is confused or dubious.

"Yes," I say curtly, still reluctant to discuss the encounter.

"In the prison?" And I hear the evident confusion in his voice.

"No—well, yes, but then she teleported us to a large, empty white space, and ..." I can tell that Josh's mind is not on what I am saying anymore. "What is it?"

"Jules," he says urgently. "We need to get Jules."

Worry floods my mind as Josh drops to the floor instantaneously. If Jules is not here, who is to say what kind of danger she might be in?

Chapter 2

I DROP TO THE floor beside Josh, and we pull on our energy to reach out to Jules. I think of her—her long black hair; her seriousness, focus, and efficiency, like Josh's and mine; her intelligence; her friendship—and I call out to her with my mind. I search for her until I feel the beat of a heart next to mine. It is slightly faster than mine, though not as fast as my heart was when I faced the Killer. Still, it is fast, and I hope that she is not in any danger.

I cling to that heartbeat, letting it intensify in my own chest and letting the rest of her being become a part of me. I feel her intensity, her focus, her mind, signifying that we are connected. If I can feel her, then she can feel me.

Suddenly, I am sucked deeper into the connection. It is

strong, and I can feel her urgency as if it were my own as she eagerly grasps for the *signal*. She is pulling us to her, and I can tell that she was eagerly looking for us to find her.

I can see through her eyes, but she is swinging her head from left to right so quickly that it blurs my view of her surroundings. I glimpse a lot of green all around her and a small waterfall that flows into a little pond surrounded by decorative rocks and pebbles. There are flowering trees and green grass everywhere.

It looks beautiful and peaceful—as if maybe Josh and I should go there—but something is not right. She is anxious, but I cannot understand why. She still pivots left and right, feverishly looking for something. This is abnormal for Jules's calm, collective demeanor, and I wonder what could have her so beside herself.

I call for her in my heart, wishing her to be here with me and Josh. As I do, I feel Josh's intangible presence with her as well, his *signal* right beside mine. I have never *signaled* someone simultaneously with someone else before. It is interesting to feel all three conscious beings at once, but I do not have time to examine it right now.

Jules begins to teleport from her location, and all of the loud busyness of the connection—the heartbeats, the thoughts, the panic, the sights—is suddenly cut off with silence and emptiness like an unexpected blow to the face. The abrupt gust of lack practically knocks the wind out of me, and my mind feels strangely empty in the sudden silence. My eyes fly open in shock.

I look at Josh, who lifts his eyes to meet mine. They are stretched wide with just as much surprise as I have. Josh is from an older age segment of students than me and Jules and has had more training at home than we have, but he has only trained a few times with *signaling*. I would imagine that he has never connected with three people before either.

Something moves in my peripheral vision. Josh and I turn to see Jules standing in front of us, cloaked in the orange-yellow light of the setting sun. The curving designs of the gray suit gracefully reflect the evening light so that she is dressed in gray-and-golden splendor, and she stands tall and unmoving while her straight black hair falls down her back. She looks like the Jules I know but with a special orange tint that makes her glow with radiance. I wonder if I looked so majestic when I arrived.

Her eyes are narrow and alert but soft. Though we are in a safe environment, Jules is still looking around for something, like she was in the greenery, and it is not for us.

"Jules," Josh says to catch her attention.

Her eyes snap down to us. "Josh! Sophie!"

"Hi, Jules," I say.

Josh and I get up from the floor.

"Are you two all right?" she asks.

"We are fine, Jules—"

"What about you?" I ask her, interrupting Josh's reply. I do not care about her question. Obviously, we are all right. I want to know what disturbed her so much in the forest. Furthermore, I would like to know how she got there, because I doubt that the prison is surrounded by something as beautiful and peaceful as that forest.

Jules turns to me with a look of fear on her face that apprehends me. Her lips part before she has the words to speak. "They were coming after me."

I worry that she means a Killer.

"Who?" Josh asks.

She looks at him and then back at me with confusion, as though it should be obvious. "Firebursts."

"Firebursts?" I relax a little. Being captured again by the Firebursts would not be good, but it is better than any of us being killed at first sight by an assassin. Then again, there is the Prophecy ...

"They know that we escaped?" Josh asks.

"Are you sure?" I cut in.

Jules looks back and forth between us. "Of course I am sure," she tells me as though insulted that I would question her judgment, but then she bashfully casts her eyes down as though uncertain of her conclusion. She looks back up at Josh. "And I am not certain if they know that we have escaped. I only know that they were chasing me. In the corridors, I found a door to a stairwell. I ran up some stairs and found an exit. I came out to a meadow on the side of a hill that merged into a forest."

I am surprised to hear that there actually is such a beautiful forest just outside the prison.

"It was not this room from the Prophecy," she acknowledges with a sweep of her arm to encompass the room that we are standing in, "but I thought that maybe it could be a place for us to gather and continue our search." As if to justify her own thought patterns to herself, she adds softly, "Better you were out of the prison in a safe environment than stuck in a seemingly endless maze, looking for a way out." She resumes speaking normally. "I was going to do a quick perimeter check to ensure that it was safe before *signaling* you two, but almost as soon as I surfaced, I noticed a group with red skin in black attire at the peak of the hill. They spotted me and started racing toward me. There was fire. I could see it off in the distance, and I could smell it too. It could not have been more than a quarter mile away from me."

At the sound of "fire," my mind flashes to the flaming eyes that I saw earlier. Perhaps I was not simply seeing a manifestation of rage. Maybe it was a sign of a *gift* to manipulate fire. Sometimes I think that I catch a glimpse of lightning in Josh's eyes right before he strikes with his *gift*. I shove the thought aside.

Jules says that she is certain they were Firebursts who were after her, but she does not appear to be sure. And she said that she saw red skin—in black clothing. I remember the black suit worn by my pursuer.

We have only witnessed red skin twice in our lives, with the exception of my last encounter. We saw it when our home was destroyed and then when we were taken captive. Both occurrences only included Firebursts. Even if the skin of Jules's pursuers was different from that sunburnt color that we have seen in the past, she may not have noticed the different shade under the pressure of a threat coming her way. The natural thing to do would be to run, and it would only be a logical conclusion that her pursuers were Firebursts. I am just not entirely certain that it was Firebursts who were pursuing her.

"I ran down the hill into the forest," she continues. "I tried to stay calm and keep a level head—to stay focused and manage my fear. I needed to have full control of myself and develop a plan, though nothing ever came to me. I thought that I heard something nearby when I reached that clearing you two found me in. There was rustling in the trees somewhere, so I abruptly came to a halt."

I recall her anxiety and fast heartbeat when we connected. She is good at staying calm, though. My heart would have been racing much faster than hers in that situation.

Jules's eyes wander to the floor as she relives the encounter in the forest. "I could not see what it was, but I knew that if I moved, or did not at least try to protect myself, it would be the end of me. I knew what the Prophecy said, but it could have been wrong. For all we know, the Prophecy could have excluded some detail of something terrible happening before we became free. The Firebursts ... they could have captured me, and then who knows what they would have done to me to bring you two back?" She stares at nothingness in silent memory of her own terror. "That was when you found me," she whispers.

Her own fears mirror the very concerns that I had. Evidently, both of us have been worried about being captured and summoning each other back into captivity. Though we were aware of the Prophecy, there were numerous possibilities that served as distractions and were more tangible than the image of an Envisionment in a crystal ball.

"It is hard to believe something when opposing forces are standing right in front of you," I comment.

Jules looks up at me, comforted by my sensitivity. As terrible as it is, I have to admit that I am glad that I was not the only one who had trouble believing the Prophecy.

My mind wanders back to Jules's pursuers, though, and I wonder just how red they were.

"Did you ever see their faces?" I ask.

Jules's expression contorts with confusion, and she shakes her head. "No, I did not see them up close, but they were red." She says it firmly, as though to put an end to my questioning. What she does not know is that I am not questioning whether the faces were red. She opens her mouth and hesitates before saying, "Maybe a little more red than usual. I do not know. I did not get a very good look at them."

She never saw their faces, and they might have been redder than the average Fireburst. They wore black outfits, and there was fire. They were not Firebursts after all. They were worse.

They were worse than what I dealt with, because I only dealt with one. Jules fled from a multitude of them.

I am in shock. I can only think of how fortunate we are that Jules ran as fast as she did and that we retrieved her when we did. If the integrity of the Prophecy were even slightly defective, Jules would not be held hostage right now. She would be dead.

I must be wearing my thoughts on my face, because Jules looks at me curiously, and Josh rests a hand on my shoulder.

"Are you okay?" he asks.

"Those were not Firebursts that were after you, Jules."

Josh removes his hand from my shoulder, secluding himself into his own thoughts and noticeably stunned by what he knows I am about to say.

"What do you mean, Sophie? What else could they have been? I was right outside of the prison."

I shake my head. "You said that you saw fire and red skin in black suits. I know that they were not Firebursts because ... I just faced someone who fits that exact description you just gave ... and it was not a Fireburst."

Jules's eyes change from a look of skepticism to one of curiosity.

"I faced a Killer, Jules ..."

Her curiosity vanishes into horror.

"Those were Killers coming after you."

"Wh-wha—how would—why would—"

"I do not know why they came after us. I just know that they did."

"I could have died," she whispers to herself.

"No. The Prophecy said that we would make it," Josh corrects her from his seclusion.

Jules looks at him as though he is crazy, and I cannot say that I disagree with her. Josh did not go through the scenarios that we did, so he does not know just how impractical the Prophecy may seem at times. I wonder if he would still quote what the Prophecy said if a Killer or even a Fireburst stood in his way.

"I suppose it turns out that some of those rumors about Killers are true," he says.

I nod.

"Could it have been the Firebursts that sent them?" Jules asks, considering the situation intensely with her arms crossed and her chin on her fist.

I am about to say that I am not sure when Josh shakes his head. "I doubt it. The Firebursts would have come after us themselves if they wanted to retrieve us. They are not known for sending others to do their work for them. I could be wrong—maybe they have a dungeon full of disposable Killers that they can dispense at their leisure, but I doubt it. Besides, Killers are only meant to kill. They do not do anything else. If the Firebursts just wanted to kill us, they would not have taken us as prisoners in the first place."

"That means that we have more people after us," Jules says solemnly.

Josh takes in a deep breath before responding. "Yes."

A wave of weariness and fear whips through my heart, and I catch it too late. I feel a small surge of my *field* leave me just as I draw the rest back in. The books in the corner by the protruding closet abruptly shift, and Josh's and Jules's heads whip pointedly toward them in alarm.

"Sorry," I utter bashfully.

The tension leaves their bodies.

"What do they want with us?" Jules wonders aloud.

"Well," Josh says, "the Firebursts wanted to eliminate our people because there were rumors of a resistance rising, but I do not know about the Killers. We probably will not be able to find out their motive until we discover who sent them. For now, we focus on being safe. And right now, we are not. We are still near the prison—no more than a couple of miles away. I just came out through an air duct and ran for a couple of miles before I saw the mansion and recognized it from the Prophecy. I came in, did a quick investigation for any immediate dangers, and *signaled* you in when I found none."

My mind flashes back to the crystal ball that came between us in the prison. Josh sat on his bed, and Jules and I stood around the ball, watching it in awe. We had heard of these predictive entities back at home, but we never personally encountered them before. Few ever have. And no one knew very much about them.

The cloudy haze in the ball cleared to zoom in on the image of a large old mansion, a rare but beautiful establishment. The mansion grew in size until the view passed through the walls and showed the three of us talking together, safe and sound, in a room—in this dark room. It barely had any light, and it had the same vacant space, maroon walls, high ceiling, dining table, books, and extravagant chandelier.

The Envisionment lasted only a few moments as the prophetic words "TODAY YOU WILL FIND FREEDOM!" were recited. The image was absorbed by the cloudy fog that it had appeared in, and the ball disappeared with a soft flash. That was it, and we knew that today was our day of escape.

It was not too difficult either. The guard had it coming. He never should have come with our rations alone—even if he was a Fireburst. We had no fear once we received the Prophecy. We were bold and daring, and we were confident. We thought that everything would be so simple and that we would be invincible. We thought that nothing could stop us and that nothing could go wrong. Oh, how naive we were. Then again, we were never harmed. Our beliefs and our confidence were the only things that were bruised—for me and Jules, anyway—and that was only by our own doubts. That was no error on the Prophecy's part.

"We are still in danger," Josh continues. "And if Killers were after you two during your escape attempts, then we are definitely not safe, because they cannot possibly be too far behind us. We need to keep moving, so we will leave this evening while the very last rays of light are diminishing."

We all look simultaneously at the light sprawling through the window. The sun is almost down, but not yet.

"We will go in a little while," he concludes.

Jules and I agree.

I have always admired his logic and efficiency—even if he is a little too serious at times, in my opinion. Jules and I can be at a loss for how to handle a situation, and Josh will recommend something that makes perfect sense. Or he will propose a logical direction to focus our minds until we have better information. He holds us together in the midst of complications, and I do not know how we could have made it this far without him. He even helps us with our training. He may be only a little older than us, but in that small gap is a plethora of tactics, adeptness, and wisdom.

We disperse. Josh returns to a sitting position on the floor with his hands resting on his knees, palms up and cradling active *bolts of electricity*. Jules goes off to the darker, empty side of the room, and I turn toward the books. Our leisure time would best be spent preparing for any battles that may come our way. We escaped just as the Prophecy said, but our home is gone, and we are all alone with two ferocious enemies coming after us. We do not have our protective parents anymore. Nor do we have our friends or our instructors to help us. And who knows what we may encounter next?

I push the thoughts aside, knowing that we do not have time or room for distractions right now. We did our share of mourning while we were prisoners. Now we need to be ready. We need to prepare for whatever will come next.

I stare at the books in the corner. I observe the size of the stack and flex my energy, which I can feel coursing through me with heat, adrenaline, and possibilities. I shuffle my fingers and fiddle with my *field* inside me, feeling its energy like liquid mingled with the blood in my veins. The pile of books is not very large. It is only a stack of five, but a couple are massive.

I relax with my arms idle at my sides, ready to train. I take a deep breath in and let it out, focusing on moving my energy slowly through my body, exercising control. I feel the energy surge throughout my body from deep within. The heat and adrenaline spread everywhere in an instant so that I cannot pinpoint the energy's location until it reaches my shoulders. Then it travels down my arms to my hands.

As the energy reaches my palms, I extend my right hand to the books in front of me and push my *force field* out. I bring my other hand up to steady and control my *field*. I feel it seeping out of my hands as I move it forward, controlling it like a muscle and feeling the environment around it like it is an extension of my skin. It flows like water slowly pouring out of me. I feel it pull at my hands as it stretches across the distance, reaching for the books. I close my eyes and focus on the constant flow of energy to my hands and the smooth flow of my *field* through them.

I feel the books through my *field* as it reaches them, and I can feel them through my hands as though my own palms were touching them. I can feel the edges of every cover, the roughness of every surface, and the ridges of every page in between. I feel everything as my *field* enwraps the books, and I can visualize the distinct sizes and textures of each book behind my eyelids better than I could see them in the dim lighting of the room. My hands, my mind, and my *field* are all one system.

I withdraw my *field* and open my eyes to see the books unmoved, still in their original positions in the pile. I guide my *field* to seep between the top two books, feeling every bump in the covers as I traverse through them. My *field* reaches free space right before it bumps into the wall on the other side of the pile. The side of my mouth twitches with satisfaction. I raise my hands slightly to elevate the top book. I weigh it in my *field*, bouncing it up and down. It weighs no more than the average book—about a pound or so. I rotate my right hand as though to turn a doorknob and flip the book upside down in my *field*. I turn my hand back and return the book to the pile.

I extend the *field* over the entire pile and lift all the books into the air, feeling the weight in my hands. I jerk them apart, and all five books fly away from each other instantaneously. They hover in the air in an uneven row as five dark silhouettes. I can barely even see their white pages. Only then do I realize just how much darker it has gotten.

"It is time to go," a soft voice says from behind me.

I arrange the books back into a pile and flip my right palm

up to carry the weight of the books in my *field*. I release my left hand and turn around to look at the owner of the voice. There is no light streaming in through the tall window anymore. There is only a soft blue haze outside. It is too dark for me to see anything more than Josh's silhouette standing behind me, and I cannot even see Jules. The sun has gone down, and only a shadow of the day's light is left in the sky. It is time to go.

Chapter 3

WE ARE DESCENDING AN old spiral staircase on one side of the mansion rather than taking the stairs that I saw outside the room we were in. It would not be wise to take the obvious way out of the mansion when we do not know what we will find outside. It is better to surreptitiously exit from a side door, where we can safely see what we are walking into and escape quietly or have the element of surprise if anyone is waiting for us.

As it turns out, the black door that I thought opened to a closet actually leads to this spiral staircase with stone walls and tight turns that make me feel like I am simply spinning around in circles. It could make a person dizzy if they descended too quickly. This is apparently how Josh got in.

I still carry a book in my *field*. I flip it and turn it in front of my face with one hand as I wriggle my fingers. It is comforting.

After numerous winding steps, we reach the wooden door at the base of the staircase. A small, shallow, arched nook sits in the base of the inner staircase wall. I open my hand to push the book into the nook and settle it on the floor. Josh opens the door, and I follow him and Jules out of the mansion.

It is dark. There is barely any light out. There is only the beautiful, soft blue haze of the evening sky, and I can just make out the first of the stars tonight. No lurking enemies appear to be waiting for us, though.

Exiting the mansion on its right flank, I look up at the building. It is big, old, and gray—and it is beautiful, just like what we saw in the Envisionment. The spiral staircase is a very narrow tower that is too small to serve as anything else. Its size certainly explains the tight curves in the staircase. It seems oddly placed. In fact, it is the only tower attached to the mansion—as though its construction was an afterthought. The mansion is decorated with large windows and a grand entrance with wide stairs and grandiose pillars that support an ornate balcony.

A large field of grass stretches out from the mansion. On either side of the grassy terrain is a thick row of short trees.

They line the lawn no more than three feet apart from each other, with different-colored leaves falling to the ground, and stretch toward a large hedge that borders the far side of the field ahead.

We are near the line of trees on the right side of the mansion. A raised plant bed runs along them, decorated with red, yellow, orange, and green leaves. Just on the other side of the hedge stands a very tall, lean tree that is barren. Its scrawny arms reach out to the sky, welcoming any promise of rain and new life—that does not appear to have come for a long time. It looks lonely with no other trees around it, and it stands taller than any of the others.

On top of it all, the sky casts its dull but beautiful blue haze on everything right before it will become dark. Once that happens, not only will no one be able to see us, but we will not be able to see anything either. We need to move quickly.

We jog swiftly but quietly across the field. The grass muffles the sound of our footsteps, and the wind is no more than a whispering breeze in the autumn atmosphere. The beautiful evening contrasts ironically with the turmoil that we have faced today.

I cannot help but wonder what sort of terror we may come to. The Prophecy promised that we would reach that room in freedom and safety, but we have already left it. We are no longer under the protection of the Prophecy's promises. So, where does that leave us now? We are on our own, alone, like that lonely, barren tree. What does that leave us susceptible to? We may escape today only to be starving tomorrow, or captured, or tortured, or killed. The Prophecy vaguely showed us that we would reach that mansion. But what happens after that? And who is to say that our escape was not for nothing, only to come to a terminal end?

I wipe the thoughts from my mind. We need to focus on survival. We will survive.

The three of us continue running, side by side. The soft breeze whisks refreshingly across my face, and I focus on the nice scenery around us—on the sensation of being free from captivity. I try to ignore the burden of knowing that we are still being hunted. I watch the trees as we jog by. They all look the same: multicolored and attractive. The red, orange, yellow, and green pass by when I see something shift among the trees. A large figure towering just below the trees manifests mysteriously from the shadows.

My first instinct is alarm at a lurking Fireburst, but his face is not red. It is a healthy tanned color. He is broad and bulky with shaggy black hair, and he wears a black, short-sleeved T-shirt that shows his muscular, tattooed arms. They are muscular because they are trained to kill, and probably tattooed to indicate whatever division he belongs to. He is dangerous, and he is after us.

"Go!"

Josh and Jules barely spare a glance at me or the intruder before they are sprinting down the lawn. I am right behind them as the stranger charges out from the shadows. I flex my *field* around us in case the stranger launches an attack. I do not know what *gift* he may possess—it may not even be something that he can project at us—but I am not taking any chances. How did he even get there among those trees? He seemed to just appear out of the shadows.

Despite the temptation, I dare not look behind us. I need to focus on moving forward and fast. I have not yet felt an attack hit my *field*, but that does not mean that I will not.

We are nearing the hedge. It is only a few yards away. If we could reach the other side of it, we could probably lose our pursuer. It is extraordinarily dense—too thick to run through. Once we are on the other side, even if the stranger has a *gift* that would enable him to quickly traverse through the hedge, we could use the cover to our advantage and launch a surprise ambush on him.

The question is, how do the three of us get to the other side of that hedge? It extends endlessly both ways, so we cannot go around it. We cannot go under it or through it either. Then I notice the barren tree and realize that there is only one option: we have to go over it.

"Hey!" I call to Josh and Jules.

They glance back at me.

I do not want to say what I am thinking out loud, or the man chasing us will hear it. I jerk my head up, gesturing to the tree on the other side of the hedge.

Josh looks up and processes my plan. He turns back and nods at me. Jules flashes a knowing smile without even looking at the tree. I suppose she was thinking the same thing.

Curiosity as to our distance from the stranger is eating away at me. I take a quick glance behind me, expecting to find our pursuer only a few feet away, but I do not see him anywhere near us. Perhaps his *gift* enables him to vanish, or perhaps this is some other kind of trick. I feel uneasy. We will have to act quickly once we reach the hedge.

I tap into something other than my *field*—something that is a different energy and is more tangible in my arm. I flex it in my forearm like a muscle as we reach the hedge. All three of us stop simultaneously with our arms up and palms out. I just hope that this emaciated tree is strong enough to support our weight.

My *branch* shoots out first. Josh's and Jules's *branches* shoot immediately after mine. Our *branches* wrap around the lonely tree's branches, and instantaneously we are yanked up before any attack or assailant reaches us. The tree is strong enough to support our weight, because it does not bend as we pull on it to soar through the air.

The wind whips across my face, and I almost feel like I am flying. We reach the peak of our flight over the hedge, and our *branches* recoil into our wrists as our trajectory carries us through the tree's branches.

I do not care about colliding with the little twigs, but I twist my body to dodge two thick branches. In my peripheral vision, I see Josh and Jules do the same, and we are falling to the green grass below. The wind rushes past me as I brace myself to land. My knees are bent, my left leg straighter than my right. My arms are out at my sides to slow my fall, and my hands are open and ready for landing.

The ground comes up lightning-fast. Before I know it, my left foot reaches the ground, and I collapse to my right foot in front, cradling the landing. My weight is thrown gracefully forward onto my hands just before my left knee would collide with the ground, and my elbows bend outward, fighting the momentum. I fear that I will crack my nose on the ground, but my body halts just as blades of grass tickle my nose. I have stopped just in time.

I automatically take inventory of my bones, particularly in my legs, as Jules and Josh land. Josh rolls once sideways on the grass and stands fluidly. He stumbles forward as Jules lands on her feet with her *branch* feeding through her wrist, attached to the tree. She must have launched it again as a grappling hook to slow her fall. I will have to learn how to land like them. Their landings do not appear as risky as mine.

Satisfied that nothing in my body is injured, I decide that I will have to train with Josh and Jules on my landings if I want to live. Fortunately, our bones and muscles are extraordinarily strong, though still susceptible to injury.

I remember the pursuer and realize that we still may not be safe. I do not know if he can pass through the hedge or if he has some other way of pursuing us. Whatever the situation may be, we need to be ready for him just in case.

I stand up as Jules retracts her *branch*. Josh has started to walk back to us when he freezes with fear in his eyes. I look at him, wondering what is wrong. Then I see what has frozen him in place, and fear courses through me so deeply and so suddenly that it almost chokes me.

The late hour casts a more eerie blue over everything now. We stand in the middle of an ever-extending strip of grass to our left and to our right. Lining the narrow field, opposite the hedge, is a barren forest with trees that resemble the one we used to cross over the hedge. Autumn leaves litter the forest floor, and despite the faint blue color in the air, nothing but bone-chilling blackness and dark shadows lurk among those trees. That is not what scares me, though. It is what stands in front of the forest and in front of the hedge. We are not the only ones on this strip.

Like eerie statues in the soft blue haze, a row of people line either side of the narrow field. About twelve stand dispersed on each side, staring at us, in all-black clothing—or what appears to be black in the dim light. They are uncanny shadows, and like the man on the other side of the hedge, they do not seem to have red skin. This confuses me. I cannot understand why they are here and why they are staring at us if they are not red-faced Firebursts or Killers. Did we interrupt something only to bring about our own demise? We are outnumbered, and we are surrounded. How are we supposed to escape them?

"Run!"

Jules and I automatically follow Josh's order. We run up the field as fast as we can, following Josh.

Everyone on our flanks closes in on us, and the four or five people at the end of the barricading lines move in to the center of the strip, blocking our escape route ahead. Maybe we will not make it through the crowd, but one thing we will do if it kills us is try, because that is who we are. We are dauntless Conquerors from the Conquest Division, and we will fight our way out of this. We have to.

Energy rigorously courses through me, looking for an outlet. There is too much adrenaline from the fear, the panic, and the anxiety. I am emotionally compromised, and I know it. The energy is banging against the confining walls of my body, and I wonder if Jules and Josh feel the same thing.

Something blue instantaneously builds up a few yards ahead to our left, confining someone in crystalline *ice*. Jules is fighting back, and her *ice* builds up faster than it ever has before. She is emotionally compromised too.

The second I notice Jules *encase* someone in *ice*, my eyes meet Josh's, and I see *electricity* in them. Yellow streaks dance across his pupils as he flings an arm to the right, in front of me. A short *bolt of electricity* flashes past me so fast I almost miss it. My brain registers it just as his other arm launches another *bolt*. My head swings to my right, following their trajectory to a man in black, who is already on the ground, and another one, who is only a couple of feet away as he is flung back by a yellow streak.

Watching the man, I notice someone gaining on us in my peripheral vision, right behind Josh. My head shoots over my left shoulder to see him clearly, and I aim my palm at him, giving a release to the accumulated energy inside me. I do not need to contain him or to try to kill him. There is no time for that. I just shove him with my *field*, and the stored energy unexpectedly throws him over ten feet into the air.

More people are coming up behind us, but they are not as close as the last person was, nor do they seem able to attack over distances like Josh, Jules, and I can. Their threat is not as immediate as others', so my attention returns to the battle ahead. We have made it past several silhouettes already. We just need to make it past a few more shadows and through the blockade of people standing ahead of us to reach open land.

Two people on my right are a foot away, and I shove them with my *field* into the dark forest. I see another two cases of *ice* form, and a couple more yellow flashes of *electricity* send people flying before I hear an aggravated, feminine growl.

"Let go of me!"

Jules!

I glance back at her only to see someone grab Josh from

behind as well. He lets out a strangled groan, and he and Jules are both squirming in their captors' arms. I am on my own to fend off the last of the silhouettes ahead of us and those behind us to get my friends back, and I falter in my advance, overburdened by the impossibility on my shoulders.

In that single moment of delay, I am already trapped. Our pursuers surround me in a crowded circle, maintaining a safe distance. They are probably apprehensive about what I may do under the pressure. They know we fight back, and I am about to release every ounce of tension in my body in a powerful blow.

We finally escaped from that dungeon in the Firebursts' base only for these people to get in our way. Now they have my friends. I am *not* happy—neither with them nor with myself. I am livid!

I fault myself, because I should have put up a *field* to protect us. I should have been smarter. Why did I not shield us? I suppose I did not think to, since no attacks were being launched at us. Or, maybe I did not think they would get close enough to grab us. Perhaps it was both. Either way, it is too late. We are no longer under the covering of the Prophecy, and as I stare into the faces of the dark silhouettes surrounding me, I realize that it is over.

Still, I will not go down without a fight. Though I am frightened, I am determined. I have a *field*, I have *branches*, and I have friends, a family, that I am willing to fight for—that I am willing to die for.

I crouch slightly and let my energy channel into my hands as our pursuers gather around. I am about to let the force blow from my hands. I can feel it brewing in my palms, practically tangible, like a small ball that I curl my fingers around.

Suddenly, something hinders me. Up close, I can truly see the faces of our pursuers. Some are male, and some are female. Some look like each other, as though they are related. Some appear young and cannot be any older than me, Josh, and Jules.

They do not look evil. They do not have the arrogant, smug smirk of a Killer or the angry, hateful look of a Fireburst. They just look like ... people ... with normal skin tones and big or small brown or blue eyes that almost look ... kind ... yet focused and intent. I imagine this is how Josh, Jules, and I must appear when we fight. They remind me of people from home ... when we had a home.

Then, I remember that these people did not come looking for us. We barged in on them. Although I do not understand why they are chasing us if they were not coming after us in the first place—

"STOP!"

Chapter 4

EVERYONE STOPS IN THEIR tracks. My body straightens of its own accord, and the brewing balls of my *force field* dissipate. The voice was so authoritative that even I am impacted by the sudden exclamation. Everyone around me stands a little straighter as well. I did not even notice that some of them were crouching.

My energy is replaced with confusion. No one is looking at me anymore. They are all looking back down the narrow field in the direction from which we came. A few quiet moments leave me wondering what is going on.

Then the crowd parts to create a narrow opening down the middle of the terrain. I notice how much the sky has darkened already. The blue haze is now nearly black. I can barely see anything. I strain to see what is happening through the gap in the crowd.

I can make out Josh and Jules at the side of the field, by the hedge, holding still in the arms of their captors. The one holding Jules is a woman with long dark hair, who appears older than us and has a dark complexion and toned arms. I can see the lines of her muscles in the diminishing light as she holds Jules's torso too tightly. Jules must have given her a hard time.

Josh is held by a man who is thickly built. He is almost twice the size of Josh, though Josh is not a small person, and his neck looks about the size of Josh's head. He is one of the few people here wearing a short-sleeved T-shirt. Almost everyone else wears a coat or some other garment with long sleeves. The captor's thick arms, wrapped around Josh's torso, are covered with tattoos—just like the pursuer from over the hedge.

Someone is approaching the narrow opening in the crowd. He enters the circle and stops once he is just inside the perimeter, leaving a few respectful yards between us.

"I am so sorry for this ... inconvenient encounter," he says as he waves his hand to encompass the scene. "This was not supposed to get so out of hand." He looks back at the man and woman holding Josh and Jules. "Let them go, please."

The man and the woman robotically release Josh and Jules,

though the woman seems a little reluctant. She looks down at Jules with a bitter expression as Jules spitefully shakes fluidity back into her limbs. Jules catches sight of the woman's unpleasant stare and glares back. Josh stands where he is, unfazed by the big, burly man standing behind him, who can hold him hostage with his bare hands. He is vigilant and focused, just like we always are when faced with predicaments, and just like these people were just a moment ago.

The authoritative man in the circle turns back to me. "Forgive us. We did not mean any harm to the three of you, Sophie."

He speaks in an uncommon formal manner for someone foreign to the Conquest Division. There are few divisions that speak in a formal dialect—and how does he know my name? He addresses me by my nickname, which has only ever been used by Josh and Jules. Everyone back at home addressed us by "Sophia," "Julia," and "Joshua," as nicknames were not commonplace, though we three tend to gravitate to them.

I stare intently at his face, trying to recall some kind of association with this man, but he does not look familiar to me. The only thing that I can put it to is that these people work for someone who is coming after us. But this man is right: these people never tried to hurt us. They grabbed Josh and Jules but immediately let them go upon this man's order. Hence, I am still mystified.

"We are a resistance against the Fireburst establishment," he continues. "Some of us are remnants of destroyed villages and communities that were ruined by the Firebursts. Others have simply chosen to leave home and join the division. We train in our training facility a while off from here, harnessing our ... *abilities*."

A resistance? It sounds too good to be true. Correction: it sounds too impossible. There actually is a resistance? It is real? I would never have guessed that anyone would actually try to challenge the Firebursts. I thought that the Resistance was only a rumor.

Frankly, the Firebursts are too rigorous. They are too dangerous. These people have to be seriously trained to plan to challenge the Firebursts. No one from home had the chance to even try to fight back, except for the attempt to defend our home. Conquest was a strong and tough division in comparison to others, such as Diligence, Love, and Strength. It had among the best chances of challenging and defeating the Firebursts, and yet even it could not defeat them.

Josh and Jules approach the circle. They stand just outside the crowd, in clear earshot to hear what the man is saying.

"When I saw the three of you on the other side of the hedge, I tried to stop you, knowing that you were headed right for the middle of our group."

So this is the man from the other side of the hedge. I only now recognize the dark silhouettes of the tattoos on his arms that I noticed earlier.

"They would not have hurt you, of course, but I did not want the three of you"—he looks back at Josh and Jules, incorporating them in the conversation—"to get a fright when you ran into the full group. I stopped chasing you, however, once I realized that I would not be able to stop you without calling out to you." He briefly glances around as he quietly says, "It is not always safe to speak around here, so close to the Fireburst Compound."

I look around as well, worried that there might be red skin lurking in the shadows or that there could be threats beyond our known adversaries in the vicinity.

He notices my sudden concern. "It's okay," he says at regular volume. "There are no dangers out tonight. I have been on patrol for the past hour or so and have not seen any. I only wanted to make sure just now. One can never be too cautious. Do not worry, though. We are safe."

He flashes a reassuring smile at me, but I do not entertain it.

I just wait for him to continue, because I do not know if I trust him.

"Anyway, I knew that charging after you would only frighten you more than I already had when I appeared among the trees. My apologies for that as well. You see, my *ability* involves blending with the winds as I please, and I was on patrol, guarding the perimeter, when I saw the three of you."

Now I understand why no one has attacked us. It is not because they do not have ... *abilities*, as the man put it. They just refused to hurt us—even though we hurt some of them. At this realization, guilt begins to creep into my heart.

"My intention was always to be sensitive to your emotions. As you were in the Fireburst Compound, I knew that it would only be reasonable for you to be a little jittery."

I feel a pang of surprise shoot through me. Not only does this man mysteriously know my name, but he knows that we were prisoners of the Fireburst Compound. I must be wearing my perplexity on my face, because he responds to it.

"You see, we received an Oracle telling us to meet the three of you here. The rendezvous did not go quite as peacefully as we had hoped, I am afraid," he says regretfully.

So that is what they are all doing here—and how this man knows my name. Josh, Jules, and I are no longer under the covering of an Envisionment, but the Prophecy still proves to be true. We escaped the Fireburst Compound today, and we are still free—free and safe ... I believe. Something light is birthed inside me aside from the guilt: hope.

"You are free to join us if you would like," the man continues. "Though the Oracle sent us here, I am not going to force you to come with us. It is your decision. My name is Walter." He graciously extends his hand to me, but I do not take it. I am still uncertain about him. There is no sense in introducing myself, anyway. He already knows my name.

The crowd widens its narrow opening in the middle of the grassy strip behind Walter, forming a scattered semicircle around us, as Josh approaches Walter. Josh, of course, is the first of us to speak.

"I am Josh," he says, introducing himself with his nickname.

Walter turns around to shake Josh's extended hand, and I hear him say, "I know." The so-called Oracle mentioned all of our names, I suppose.

Behind Josh, I see Jules, who looks firmly planted. She refuses to move, but she is relaxed. She leans on one leg, and her arms are crossed instead of at her sides and ready for action. I cannot see her face in the darkness, but judging by her stance, she is not entirely convinced—though she is not entirely unconvinced either. Jules is assessing the situation. That is about as close to a yes as anyone will ever get from her in times of uncertainty such as this.

I do not see anything wrong with this organization. As unsure as I may be right now, clearly they have no intention of hurting us. Otherwise, they would have retaliated when we attacked them. If nothing else, they are a safe group to join for now. I approach Walter on his right, across from Josh.

"Walter," I say, looking at Josh for any sign of opposition to what he knows I am about to say. He tilts his head down in the slightest nod, a subtle movement that only a closely knit unit like Josh, Jules, and me could communicate with. Walter looks at me just as my eyes leave Josh. Up close, I notice that Walter's eyes are brown and almond-shaped, catching the faint light of the moon that twinkles like a sparkle caught in his pupils. His dark hair is long enough to hover just over his hairline and smoothly ripple over his forehead in the wind. "We would like to join you."

He beams down at me with a smile that gleams as white as the moon. "Wonderful!" he declares.

He turns to look at Jules, and his grin fades. He is not looking at Jules, though. He stares into nothingness as he looks at the mess we have made, particularly the icy statues gleaming in the moonlight. The people that Josh attacked are now getting up. They were not hit with anything more than minor *bolts of electricity* that left them twitchy for a few minutes. I know—I have felt them before in training sessions. Recipients recover from them quickly. Josh never puts his *ability*—I really like that word—on full power unless absolutely necessary.

I wonder what happened to the people who I shoved with my *field*, particularly the one I shoved several feet into the air. I have not heard any screams, so perhaps he has an *ability* that saved him from any major injuries. Jules's victims, on the other hand, are another story. I have not yet come across an *ability* that can overpower hers—not even *fire*. It has always left me in wonder, but it is also very dangerous.

The truth is, however, it could be worse. It is not only Josh who does not attack people at full intensity unless absolutely required to; it is all three of us. I could squeeze a person to death with my *field*, and Jules could thoroughly freeze a person from the inside out. We still need a lot of training, but we are already very effective. We never want to hurt anyone, though. Just because we can does not mean that we will.

Still, we hurt these people. And the guilt makes me cringe inwardly as I see the damage that we have done, but Josh picks up the messy pieces of the situation with a gentle hand on

Walter's shoulder as though they are old friends.

"The electric shocks were not too bad, Walter," Josh says. "They should wear off soon."

Walter nods in understanding, but he stands frozen, staring at the icy statues that glow in the moonlight in a way that I struggle not to identify as beautiful, for Walter's sake. Already, in these few moments of exchange, I can see his care for these people. He has not said it, but it is clear that he is a leader—if not *the* leader—of this organization. And he is connected to every single one of its members. When they hurt, he hurts. When they mourn, he mourns. When they succeed, he succeeds. It reminds me of a sweet little community that is actually stronger than a community. It reminds me of a family that has been through difficult times and has grown into an unbreakable bond of unity, like Josh, Jules, and I did.

"They are not frozen, Walter," Josh continues. "They are only trapped in *ice*. They can be broken out."

"These warriors would be able to find their way through a sheet of ice if they were alive." Walter does not sound upset but saddened and weary—and something else more intense. Perhaps guilty for bringing them here in the first place. I guess he really does understand our intentions of self-defense if he is not angry or even distrustful of us while believing we have just killed his companions, though we really did not.

I step forward and gently place a hand on his arm. "Walter, he is right. There is not an ... *ability* that I have seen yet that can break through Jules's *ice*." It feels weird to reiterate Walter's word back to him. It shows that I am already being influenced by him, and it makes me feel vulnerable. However, perhaps it is exactly what is needed to reassure him.

Something changes in Walter's face for a moment before he looks down at me. "Then how can you tell me that they can be broken free?"

"Jules can manipulate water," Josh explains before I do. "She can make *water*, *ice*—control it, even."

"And she can transform water through the phases," I add. Walter looks bewildered.

"Jules?" Josh calls, abruptly pulling her from deep thought as she stares at the ground. Her eyes shoot up at him, and he slightly tilts his head in the direction of the *ice* statues that line the narrow field along the hedge. "Would you?" he hints.

She follows his gaze and suddenly jumps into action, purposefully striding toward the entrapped people, as though she just remembered something important. She touches the tip of her index finger to the peak of the case of *ice* nearest her. As she moves on to the next thick, deep blue statue, the first case cascades in on itself like a falling curtain, avoiding its hostage. The person inside is a man, who looks around in wonderment, as if he had gone to sleep and awoken in a foreign land.

Beside me, Walter looks surprised and impressed. I struggle to keep from smiling in amusement. It is truly a sight to behold, even for me, having seen it time and time again. I can only imagine what it must be like for Walter, who is seeing Jules's *gift* for the first time.

I look back down the narrow field to see the man now surrounded by steamy mist from the melted *ice* as Jules thaws the second case. The woman inside gasps as if she has been without air inside the blue walls. It seems a little dramatic to me. Then again, I knew I was going to be set free when Jules *encased* me in training, and she was not empowered by being emotionally compromised when she did it either. This may be different from what I have experienced.

I cringe as it occurs to me that this cannot look good to Walter, but I look up to see that he does not appear to be disturbed. Rather, he appears relieved that everyone is alive and, though a little cold, well.

The woman collapses in a cloud of cold mist while shuddering and cradling her arms to her chest, trying to get warm. Someone from the crowd rushes over to her, kneeling beside her and placing their hands on her back and cradled arms until she slowly stops shuddering. The person must have concluded that she is too cold and discombobulated to consider moving out of the cold mist.

By now, the last two *ice* cases, farther along the field, are also defrosted, leaving behind two new pillars of icy mist. Jules seems to be talking to the two newly liberated silhouettes—apologizing, perhaps—which convinces me to do the same.

"I am sorry that we lashed out at all of you, Walter."

He looks down at me with eyebrows drawn together in puzzlement. He smiles, though, and says, "There is no reason to apologize."

Josh looks back at us, rejoining the conversation. I open my mouth to respond to Walter, but he continues.

"You three have had a rough time, I am sure. I do not blame you for defending yourselves. It would be foolish not to be alert and defensive."

I close my mouth. There is nothing to say after that. He is right. We were snatched off the side of the road after our home was destroyed and thrown into a torture chamber by the very same beasts who ripped our home and everything else we loved away from us. We escaped, only to be faced by Killers and have new enemies chasing after us while darkness rapidly approaches, hindering us from seeing dangerous threats that may lurk in the night. And we are no longer under the safe covering of the Prophecy since it has already happened. Anyone who has been through as much as we have and is not vigilant is foolish.

Walter does not say it, but I can see the relief in his eyes that everyone is okay. He turns back to the defrosting individuals.

Josh meets my gaze, and I see his fascination with this community. It shows in his eyes for a split second before he turns back to Jules. She has already come back up the narrow plain to the first two people she liberated and is finishing her short conversation with them.

The other two defrosted people come to the group, cradling their arms and shivering. Perhaps the woman liberated second was not being dramatic after all. I am sure that the wind does not help. It may not be particularly strong or very cold, but when these people are already cold, the slightest breeze must feel like an ice storm. As they walk to the group, some people welcome them with embraces of warmth while the rest of the crowd watches in silence.

"Sophia?"

I halt at the familiar sound of my full first name, and I turn to the soft voice that I somehow seem to recognize. A small girl approaches me from the center of the semicircle. In the moonlight, I can see her dark hair and big, curious brown eyes, which scan my face in a familiar way that takes me back to life at home.

Education was not a very complex system in Conquest. There were a few core subjects that covered combat, strategy, culture, computational applications, history, and the sciences. Combat and strategy were the most important.

One day, a couple of years ago, a small girl in my segment began to stare at me frequently. She sat just ahead of me at a desk to my right while we were instructed in computational applications and looked too young and bubbly, with short black hair, to be older than twelve years of age, even though she was.

I began to understand the lessons after months of failing exams and simulations of the subject, and she kept turning her head back to look at me every few minutes just as I started to understand them. It was distracting and annoying. It felt like someone thwarting my progress and celebration. I tried to ignore her at first, but she persistently did it. Just as I began to understand something that would normally confound and irritate me, this girl would interfere with her intrusive stares.

Eventually, I had enough. I looked at her to find her big

brown eyes studying me as though she were trying to decipher a complicated puzzle. Intending to be discreet to avoid trouble with the stern instructor at the front of the room, who wore dull gray clothes and her hair in a neat gray bun, I mouthed "What?" in annoyance at the girl.

She jumped with a start and turned her attention back to the front of the room. It was bizarre, but at least she left me alone. Things were quiet with her for a few days after that, and I had a miserable time trying to grasp the lessons again.

After a while, though, something happened. I started to understand the lessons again, and of course, the girl resumed pestering me with her invading stares. Frustrated and annoyed, I intercepted her in the hallway right after we were released from the room and demanded to know what her issue was. She looked frightened by my outburst, as if she feared that I would hurt her. She nervously explained that her *gift* allowed her to make things clear in people's minds and worked best when she looked directly at someone. She knew that I was having trouble with the lessons, and she was only trying to help me. That explained the sudden epiphanies I had begun to have. This girl was not ruining my success; she was creating it.

My heart flooded with guilt. I apologized to her and asked her forgiveness for my reaction.

"My name is Sophia," I said, offering my hand to her.

Rather quickly her countenance changed from one of fear to one of glee. She took my hand and shook it cheerfully. "Delia," she said with a beaming grin.

We were good friends from that moment on … until everyone in Conquest was killed except for me, Josh, and Jules—or what we thought was everyone but the three of us. I am presently looking at another survivor from Conquest.

"Delia?" I am in disbelief. I guess someone from home made it to the rumored resistance after all.

"Hi." She smiles at me.

Something is different about her, though. I can even see it in the dim moonlight. Her grin used to be bright, practically blinding. Now it is reserved, and she does not seem about to bounce everywhere with peppy energy. She is so … grounded now. And she appears older. Her hair is longer. Her skin is tanner. And rather than appearing to be twelve, she appears twenty-four. Even her stance carries greater confidence and assurance. Everything about her has changed but for her size and her eyes. She is still small with big brown eyes that seem to search deep into my soul. Immediately I know that I could recognize them anywhere.

Still, I cannot get my mind off the fact that there is someone else from home … still alive … here … in a resistance. I am baffled. Not to mention the fact that this is Delia who is with the Resistance. Delia … in a resistance. I could never imagine it, even though we were both born into a warrior division like Conquest.

"How did you … I mean … when did you—"

"They found me not too far from Conquest," she explains.

At the name of our home, Josh comes to my side to hear Delia. She does not look in his direction, though. She stares off into the distance, deep in recollection.

"I was devastated," she continues. "My parents were dead. I watched them die—burned to death … I had no choice." Her voice begins to crack.

"They had us tied up. Our hands and our feet were useless. I would have jumped into the fire to try to save them. I would have done anything. I did not care, but they had my little brother. They held Timothy and threatened to set him on fire too if I even budged, but only if I budged … right there in our living room. All my parents kept saying was 'Save Timothy! Save Timothy! We love you! Save Timothy!' … They did not even care about their own lives. They just wanted us to survive—"

She breaks off, and tears twinkle in her eyes in the moonlight. She had to face the Firebursts personally while Josh, Jules, and I were sent down hidden passageways by our parents to meet at a site predetermined by our parents in case of emergencies. The door to my family's passageway was in the floor of our kitchen. Our families fought off the fires and those who started them so that the three of us could escape. We were still caught in the end, but at least we had a chance.

Delia had no chance of escaping. She did not have the hope of survival that we did—for her or for her loved ones—and I cannot help but analyze how much these circumstances have changed her. Even her speech is different from how we were brought up as Conquerors.

Delia suddenly sucks in a breath, shooting her eyes back up at me as though startled back into the present. "They killed him anyway," she says, recovered from her memories. "First chance I got, I grabbed a shard of glass, cut my rope bonds loose, *clouded* someone's mind to confound them, and I ran. I ran until my feet ached, and then I ran some more. Through the forest, down some paths ... That's when these guys found me." She briefly glances at Walter with a small smile.

I am speechless. I race through my mind, searching for something to say, but I cannot find anything.

"Excuse me, ladies," Walter politely cuts in, coming around

on my right, "but we should probably get going. It is dark, and we have a bit of a distance to go before we reach safety. There will be plenty of time to catch up, though." He smiles reassuringly at me and turns around to lead the crowd along the narrow plain, back in the direction from which we ran.

I can barely see anything in the darkness of the night, but I see that no one is farther down the field anymore except for Walter. I guess they all joined the crowd while I spoke with Delia. I follow Walter, and the rest of the crowd begins to move as well. However, I notice the direction that Walter is heading, and I freeze. He is walking diagonally across the field toward the dark forest on the side opposite the hedge.

I feel an arm wrap around mine. "Come on," Josh encourages as he drags me on.

I continue walking, submitting to his cajolement. We meet Jules, who never entered the crowd of people but stayed just outside it, and we walk together. I watch Walter, wondering if this forest is really as terrifying as it looks. In the darkness, it looks even more terrifying, because nothing is visible but for a few silhouettes of certain tree trunks. It is filled with absolute blackness now.

Walter stops at the edge of the forest and swiftly waves his hand above him in a broad arc. A blue light shoots up from the arc he makes in the air and expands to the ground, spreading to form an oval that contains a warped view of the forest standing behind it. Walter steps forward into the warped image, and he is gone.

I slow my pace again, stunned beyond what words can describe. This time, Josh does not resist my hesitation. Everyone in black jogs past us to the warped oval window. Upon passing, Delia briefly touches my arm and smiles reassuringly. Then she also jogs to the oval while the three of us watch in surprise and uncertainty.

The last of the Resistance members pass us, jogging to the oval window. Josh, Jules, and I are the last ones. I stare down the narrow field, wondering if we should make a run for it. Walter said that joining the Resistance is our decision, but I do not know that he meant it. I do not know that they would not force us to stay if one day we decided to leave. And I do not know that we are really safe with these people. These Resistance members must be powerful, highly trained individuals. Warriors, Walter called them. They seem genuine, but I do not know if we should take the risk.

In my peripheral vision, I notice a red trick of light coming over the hedge in the distance. It is only a small speck. I try to focus my vision through the darkness. It looks like a bird, but something is different about it.

My attention is pulled away from it when Jules suddenly picks up her pace as the last of the Resistance members go through the oval window. I suppose she is finally convinced ... surprisingly. I wonder what has caused her to be so persuaded.

Nonetheless, Josh and I automatically let go of each other and follow her lead, racing to the blue-bordered oval. Like magnets, we are connected to each other. If one of us moves, we all move. We stick together.

Jules is just ahead of us and causes a shimmer in the oval as she goes through it. Josh and I enter right behind her.

Chapter 5

I PUSH THROUGH A soft, cool liquid that is thick and elastic. The substance engulfs me with a slight resistance to my movement like water, and the coolness feels good on my skin. I am wrapped in it as it softly presses against my body. The silver waves dance all around me like underwater sunrays that move in no particular pattern. It is beautiful.

Ahead, something dark rapidly approaches me before I can even realize that I should be alarmed. Before I know it, I am in the dark night of the real world again. Jules is right in front of me, and Josh is beside me. The crowd of Resistance members stands in front of us, beginning to follow Walter onto a road that runs perpendicular to us.

Scattered under our feet from behind us are leaves. I turn

around to see what we are standing next to, and my heart leaps in shock as I take a few steps away and flex my *field* in my hands. There is no sign of the silver substance, the blue light, or a warped image in an oval. Whatever passage we came through is no longer here. There is nothing but pitch-black darkness that even the moon cannot shine through. Only a few slivers of certain trees are visible. It is the dark forest that we were near on the narrow field. Either Walter has just led us through a hidden passageway through the forest, or he made us skip it entirely ... somehow.

Josh notices my reaction and follows my gaze to the forest. He also seems surprised, but not by the threatening appearance of the forest. He seems curious as to how we got to the other side of it through a lake of silver.

I look back to the moving crowd and observe the rest of our surroundings. On the other side of the road is a few yards of rough land before it drops over a short cliff. It overlooks an ocean of twinkling water that reflects the moon and its garden of stars. The destination of the road is very apparent. In the distance on our right is an immense building—a dark castle or mansion—that stands tall and proud, with multiple grand towers. I cannot distinguish the road from the rough land over a distance in the dark, but I can see that the cliff grows taller as the path winds and swivels more and more up to the huge edifice, which stands on the edge of the cliff that towers high above the water.

A shadow turns back from the crowd of moving silhouettes and comes back to me and Josh. I did not even realize that Jules had started walking already.

"Are you two coming?" she teases.

I am surprised by her eager acceptance of these people, but I have no intention of running away, especially now that our only alternatives are miles of endless water or a dark forest that makes me uneasy.

"Yes," I say.

"Of course," Josh chimes in, turning from the forest.

Jules smiles and walks next to me. We draw near to the crowd but stay on the outskirts. I fight the urge to constantly glance at the forest, terrified that a Killer or a Fireburst might leap out of the dark shadows at any moment. I need a distraction.

"You seem oddly convinced of these people," I say to Jules.

She smirks and speaks in a soft whisper. "No. I just do not see how they can be any worse than stumbling across Fire-bursts or Killers in the middle of the night."

She has a point. If we had decided to go on our own, some-where along the way we probably would have been caught.

Even if these people are dangerous, they cannot be half as bad as the danger of either one of our current enemies. Against the Firebursts and Killers, we would barely stand a chance. The Resistance may be training against the Firebursts, but just how trained and dangerous can they possibly be?

Besides, we have nowhere else to go. Perhaps we could try to wander back to the vicinity of where Conquest used to be and find another division to settle in, but who knows where that is from here? We were unconscious for the entire journey to Fireburst territory.

My mind flashes back to when they found us on the road, leaving our destroyed home, knowing that our families and friends were all dead. We left the hidden steel hideout, thinking that the Firebursts were gone, only to be suddenly surrounded by taunting enemies and suffocating fire. I pull myself back to the present and think of Delia when she was lost in her horrifying memories.

"I guess you are right," I acknowledge, staring at the road.

Jules takes my hand and gives it a reassuring, firm squeeze. I look at her and see the message in her eyes: *Do not forget who we are—who you are. Situations may be complicated, but we can handle them. We were born, raised, and trained to handle opposition and to push against the grain, because even if things do not turn out the way that we want them to, we will have done our part as Conquerors. It is not the situation. It is how we handle it. That is what we were taught.*

I smile at her to let her know that I understand and that I am all right. She lets go of my hand.

I realize that Josh has been quiet for a while. He is somewhere deep in his thoughts. Truly, we all are. He catches me looking at him and smiles as though he has just forgotten everything that was on his mind. He seems okay, so I do not pursue it. My attention reverts to the army of dark-cloaked soldiers in front of us as we traverse the road that leads to the mansion ahead. As we walk, I recall the red bird that I saw over the hedge, and a thought occurs to me.

"What did Walter mean when he said that place is not always … safe … to speak in?" I ask, emphasizing the word that he used.

Jules opens her mouth to speak but releases her accumulated breath with puffed cheeks, at a loss for words. She shakes her head, about to say that she does not know, when Josh intercedes.

"The Firebursts have a special security system," he says. "Some of us learned about it in advanced training back home."

My heart aches at the word "home," but I push it aside to listen to Josh.

"They do not have guards or anything of that sort. They use things that you would not normally suspect—creatures of nature, like birds and squirrels, only they do not use real animals as spies. They create their own—probably with the help of someone who has a *gift* allowing them to do it—and make modifications to them. The spies can record what they see, hear, smell, taste, and touch. They replicate it for their masters, whether by producing an object with the same characteristics or by simply imitating what they detected.

"They are intelligent. They can decipher what is out of place and worth reporting to the Firebursts. Their modifications go beyond their internal functionality, though. They are ... externally enhanced as well. It varies. Usually, it is meant for defensive and offensive tactics: a chipmunk with sharper claws, a rabbit that runs abnormally fast ... Some of the modifications may even resemble *gifts*."

It is a terrifying thought that even the simplest of things can be a threat. As if we did not have enough to worry about already. And listening to Josh's list of possible modifications, I think about the red bird. "What kinds of modifications could a bird have, would you say?"

"Well, it is not exactly precise, Sophie. It could be anything—even a trait that is shared with another animal. They could fly abnormally fast, have smaller wings, have huge wings ... They could breathe fire, for all I know—"

My eyes fly up to Josh. That is it. That is what was so different about the red bird over the hedge. It did not breathe fire, but it did have fire. I briefly saw it and thought that I was imagining things in the darkness, but it was not a trick of my eyes. It was fire. Fire was emanating from the bird's wings, from its tiny torso, and most of all, it was emanating from its tail, leaving a trail of flames. Its body was fire—small but deadly. It is a good thing that the silver passage we came through closed behind us, or that bird could have followed us here. Then who knows what would have happened?

I check behind me to ensure that there is no sign of a little red flame. It would be clearly visible in the dark. To my relief, I see nothing.

"What is it?" Josh asks.

"I believe that I saw one of those birds earlier. It was after the majority of the Resistance had gone through that silver passageway. I saw it fly over the hedge a distance away down the field." I recall that Walter said we were safe. He did not lie. He just was not present when a spy did eventually come.

Josh looks concernedly at me. "How far away was it? Is it here? Did it come through with us?" He sounds frantic. Both he and Jules spin around, swinging their heads back and forth, trying to find the bird—the spy.

"No, no, no. It is not here," I assure them. "And it was a ways off by the hedge. It could not have come through. Besides, I checked."

They both calm down to think intently about this, and I understand why. The spy was not there to see us conversing with the Resistance, but if what Josh said about Fireburst spies is true, and it saw the three of us enter that passage, it could give our adversaries more information about us than we want them to have.

"We need to speak to Walter," Jules says firmly. "We need to know exactly how familiar the Firebursts are with the Resistance and to learn of Walter's history with these 'spies.' If they are familiar with him, they could already have information about this organization, causing a level of vulnerability that we need to be made aware of. Not to mention the precarious location of this castle. It is practically right next to the Fireburst Compound. How far did you say that vacant mansion was from the compound, Josh? A couple of miles? This place is a leap over a hedge and a forest away from that mansion, and we already have the Firebursts and Killers searching for us. This could be severe for us."

Jules is panicking, but it only makes sense. She just faced a whole army of Killers without even realizing it, and we have been constantly on the move. We just had the smallest inkling of relief, only for it to be snatched away again by a possible death sentence.

Distracted by the Resistance and deciding whether to trust them—and seeing Delia, a treasured memory from home—I momentarily released the fears that we had not too long ago. I carelessly let go of the concerns and the vigilance that have served to keep us alive thus far. Now everything seems to be heaping back up again instantaneously. Again, we are carrying the burden of the world on our shoulders when all that I want to carry is the weight of my own *force field* and a small object that I twirl around just above my hand for the fun of it, just as I did while exiting the abandoned mansion.

"We will speak with him tonight," Josh says, gesturing for Jules to calm down.

I look at the majestic building ahead in despair, longing to be inside. I do not want to be outside, where who-knows-what could see us and open up another door of concerns that will rip something else away from us. All that we have left is each other and a remnant of home in a girl who I know but Josh and Jules do not. Aside from that, the only thing left to be taken away from us is what we carry inside us. We only have the hope, the training, the love and care, the diligence, the Conqueror, the warrior ... Everything else was taken from us. We cannot afford to lose anything else, and losing each other is not even an option. We will not allow it. I want to get inside and deal with this situation immediately. Thankfully, we are at the gate of the mansion.

"Good. We are here," Jules comments impatiently.

"Come on." Josh holds my hand, and I am grateful for his comforting gesture. It is a reminder of something that is not ruined and that we will not allow to be stripped away.

Chapter 6

W E WALK UNDER A black wrought-iron archway that stands almost eight feet tall. Bordering the structure are thick cement walls that stand almost as high. Past the entryway, the path takes us through a large front lawn decorated with figures, but I cannot discern what they are in the dark. Against the front of the building, to the left, are stairs that descend to an enclosed stone passageway. There must be a lower level. My thoughts automatically conjure a dungeon, and I feel uncomfortable.

The road leads straight to three steps at the entrance of the mansion. The doors are massive, with archaic markings in picturesque curves and patterns. Walter ascends the steps. I cannot see what he does to open the door, assuming that they do not simply leave the front entrance unlocked, but one of the doors opens. Artificial light pours out through the growing gap and illuminates the steps and a portion of the lawn. Walter walks in, trailed by the rest of the procession. The building towers over us, reaching infinitely high into the dark, twinkling sky. Josh, Jules, and I ascend the steps and enter through the doors.

It is bright, and my eyes have to adjust. As they do, an elaborate chandelier comes into view. It hangs from the ceiling at least twenty feet high, casting a golden glow over the tiled floor and the two staircases that curve along the sides of the space to the second level. Stretching across the peak of the staircases and beyond is a balcony framed by small archways. Between the staircases is an extravagant golden statue. The walls are white, and a few are red, but they all glow gold from the radiance of the chandelier. To our right on the ground floor is an archway leading to what appears to be a lounge area. To our left, another archway leads somewhere out of sight. All that I see is a white wall forming a bend in the walkway.

This place is spacious, which does not surprise me after seeing it from the outside. However, it is very well kept, unlike the forsaken mansion that we just left. Regardless, I am too distraught to be impressed. There are too many things on my mind.

Josh and Jules examine the mansion as well, though they do not seem impressed by it either. They both look around with uninterested eyes, and I bear witness to their disposition. This place feels like nothing more than a beautiful grave to lie in.

The Resistance members disperse in chatter and head in various directions. Some go upstairs; some go through the archway on our right; and some activate and pass through hidden doors in the walls between the staircases and under the balcony. There are so many passageways.

My mind flashes back to the Fireburst Compound and its never-ending arrangement of pathways. There is an endless assortment of directions that one can take in this place. No one goes through the archway to our left, though.

The bright light clearly illuminates the Resistance members and their black attire. Glancing at them as they quickly scatter, I observe their black pants, their fitted shirts, and their black footwear.

Walter stands ahead of us, facing us as the crowd disappears. I will let Jules speak first. I am sure that she is eager. She is the most outspoken of the three of us.

Walter approaches us, hands clasped behind his back, as the last couple of people leave the space. "You three can follow me to your room. I'm afraid you will have to share tonight on such short notice, but tomorrow we should be able to find you separate bedrooms."

He turns around to walk us to our room, but we have our own plans for tonight.

"Walter, we need to discuss some things first," Jules says.

I am impressed that she has kept it in as long as she has, allowing Walter to finish speaking.

Walter turns back to us. He does not appear threatened or offended by Jules's slightly demanding tone, but I do not care for once. I am in complete agreement with Jules here, and I am sure that Josh is too.

Without question or objection, Walter nods. "Come with me."

He turns and walks to the archway on our left. We follow him through the seemingly forbidden archway that no one else even glanced at and step into a narrow white hallway that immediately turns right. Walter takes us down the small hall, which is brightly lit by ceiling lights spaced at consistent intervals. The hallway is tight and forces us to walk in single file behind Walter: Jules, me, and then Josh. The corridor is so narrow that I cannot see past Walter and Jules.

A banister intercepts the wall on our left. Like a balcony, it looks out over what must be the one place in this building that has no lights on. The banister borders the narrow corridor that we walk through and trails down a narrow staircase into the unknown space below.

"What does that staircase lead to, Walter?" I call over Jules.

There is a pause before he answers, and I wonder why.

"It leads to a room that even I do not go into. It is an area of seclusion and valuable treasure that is off-limits in this mansion. No one is permitted to enter it."

I raise my eyebrows in surprise. If it is so secretive, why would he bring us, newcomers, right by it? He does not even know us. He cannot possibly trust us so much that he is willing to lead us right by a place that he does not want anyone to enter.

Before long, the hallway ends, opening to a round chamber at the end of a tunnel. It is bright, just like everywhere else in this mansion. The walls are white, and a rectangular block carrying purple cushions and throw pillows protrudes from the far wall on the right, serving as a sort of lounge sofa. To the far left is a wooden desk near the wall, facing us, and a love seat sits against the wall across the room from us, by the desk. Between the lounge sofa and the love seat is a protrusion in the wall that runs from the floor to the ceiling, slightly dividing the two sides of the room and forming a side of the lounge sofa. At the mouth of the corridor, on either side of us, are pedestals topped with graceful little statues of people dancing.

It occurs to me that this mansion is filled with luxurious, precious items, such as the chandelier, the statues, the throw pillows—the mansion itself—which are all rare and special commodities.

Josh, Jules, and I have only come across such culture in educational sessions at home, and I cannot even enjoy it right in front of me, because all I can think about is the fact that at any unsuspected moment, we could be knocked off our feet again and stripped down until there is nothing left in us. Firebursts or Killers—I do not know which one is worse: agonizing torture or agonizing death. One would think that death would be preferable, but considering the unique ways that each party breaks you, it is hard to choose one—especially when I wish for neither to occur with every fiber of my being.

"Well," Walter says as he sits at the desk and gestures for us to have a seat. Josh sits on the arm of the love seat, farthest from the desk, allowing me and Jules to settle on the cushions of the furniture. "This is a complex situation for the three of you, I am sure. I was actually planning to speak with you in the morning, thinking that you must be drained after ... the series of events you have gone through. I wish to speak with you about a few things briefly, though."

Jules opens her mouth to interject, but Walter softly holds a hand up.

"Please, let me just say a few things first."

Jules reluctantly settles down in the love seat.

"You three have been through a lot, and I understand that. It has not been easy. We came after you once we received word that we ought to. I said that it is your decision as to whether you want to stay with us. I meant it, and I still do now. However, understand that your best chances are with us. You have every reason to be defensive and apprehensive. As I said earlier, you would be unwise not to be. Just be sure to consider your options carefully. If the Firebursts are after you, you are not safe. No one is safe anyway, let alone when the Firebursts are pursuing them specifically. You are all very well trained, and I am sure that you do not need to hear me say that. However, you are no match for them. You need intensive training, preparation, enhancements—a number of things that we provide here and are willing to share with you.

"Truth be told, I do not know why the Oracle told us to go after the three of you. None of us do. We cannot even say where it came from, but what we do know is that we did our part. Now, what you decide to do from here is completely up to you, so long as you keep the location of our headquarters confidential. I trust you enough to let you go without having your memories altered.

"Also, know that if you stay here, you must abide by the same rules as everyone else. Places that are off-limits to everyone else will remain off-limits to you as well. There are no exceptions. Schedules, training, expectations—they will all apply to you as they apply to everyone else. You can take as much time as you need to decide whether you wish to stay, but as long as you are here, you must follow the protocol of this organization. I just wanted to place that in front of you before you make any rash decisions."

"Walter, we—"

"We are not sure that staying here is safe for us," Jules interrupts Josh.

Walter looks concerned but maintains an open ear. Even in the midst of my own terror, I cannot help but observe his calm, peaceful, and seemingly understanding responses to everything. "And why is that?"

"You mentioned that it is not always safe to speak by the Fireburst Compound," Josh says, "even at that distance from the compound to that hedge you found us at. Is that correct?"

Walter nods.

Josh bites his lip. "You were referring to their spies, were you not?"

Walter seems to lose peace at the sound of this. "Yes, their security system—or any wanderers or bystanders nearby. ... How do you know about their spies?" he inquires, wincing in curiosity and astonishment. "And why do you ask?"

I am about to answer when Jules does so first. "Sophie spotted one over the hedge while we were all entering that passageway you made. It seems that it did not come through, but we do not know exactly how much it saw."

She completely overlooked Walter's initial question. I feel a minor smirk inside me, because I know that she did not want us to answer it. She feels that it is none of his concern and completely irrelevant to the situation, and to be honest, she is right.

Walter considers this, and I am glad that Jules restrains the multitude of questions that she has for him. A few quiet moments pass before he answers. "Even if the spy captured enough footage worth reporting to the compound, they cannot find us."

"What do you mean, they cannot find us?" Jules demands. "We are next door to them! We cannot be more than four miles away."

Oh no. Jules is getting frantic. As I turn to her, hoping to calm her down, I notice that Walter looks confounded. "Jules," I say softly, touching her arm with care and giving her the same reminder of who we are as she gave me earlier. We have to stay calm. Otherwise, we act based on our emotions. We would be unfocused and ineffective, and we could activate our *abilities* unintentionally. We have to keep level heads.

Jules seems annoyed, but she concedes. She takes a deep breath and tries to calm down.

At the same time, Walter realizes something. I can see the epiphany on his face as he, still gently, responds, "You think we are right next to the Firebursts because of that forest outside."

We are all silent. It was not a question but a statement of realization—one that was not of belittlement, thankfully. I do not know whether Jules could take the smallest tinge of provocation at the moment. She is already at her boiling point.

"I am so sorry. I should have explained this to you," Walter says. "First of all, you have probably never been to these parts before, seeing as they are so close to the compound and you are very young. Not to mention the fact that you are all the way from Conquest." I am surprised that he knows where we are from. "So let me inform you. Firstly, there are several of forests around here. You see them frequently. Some are safer than others, but there is a substantial number here. Secondly, we are relatively near the compound, I suppose. Yes."

Jules tenses.

"But not as close as you think," he reassures us. "The forest that you saw just outside of these headquarters is not dangerous—unless you are afraid of occasional wolves, but that is really the extent of it."

I consider wolves. I can definitely handle wolves. We all can. They are a welcome challenge in comparison to the mess that we have been dealing with for some time now.

"The forest that we found you by," Walter says, "is a dangerous one, filled with countless fears, horrors, and atrocities. Even Firebursts tend to steer clear of those lands."

A soft shiver runs down my back.

"The forest just outside of these headquarters neighbors the one that is by the hedge," he continues. "They are separated by a strip of land not unlike where we found you, though it is wider. Also, understand that these forests are expansive, spanning millions of square miles."

Tension leaves Jules's body, and she becomes more relaxed than I have seen her in a while.

"Even if the Firebursts—or anyone else, for that matter—came into this vicinity, they would not be able to get to these headquarters. We are cloaked inside of a *shield* as well as a *cloak of invisibility*." He examines the surprise that I am sure is on all of our faces. "We have some very gifted and well-trained people here."

I suppose so, I think.

"So, as you can see," Walter says, "we are very well protected here, and as I said earlier, they cannot find us. Besides, no one even knows our location. Everyone who has ever known anything about us has joined us and is still here to this day. There are no outsiders aware of us or our location. You three would be the first, and probably the only, to leave."

"So, you would really just let us go if we wanted to leave … just like that?" Josh says.

I guess Josh is just as mystified by that offer as I am.

"Yes," Walter answers. "As I said before, I trust you."

"But why?" Josh asks. "It is completely illogical. You do not even know us."

"Or anything about us," Jules quickly adds under her breath. Though she is wrong, because he knows what division we are from, and I wonder how he does. I am guessing that either the Oracle or Delia informed him, but I really cannot know for sure.

"No, but would the Oracle instruct us to come after you only to the demise of this organization and all the people in it?"

"But you said you do not even know where the Oracle came from," Jules protests. "What if it came from someone trying to sabotage the Resistance? What if it came from the Firebursts or Killers—or who knows who else could have sent it? Even if it did come from a safe source, you do not know why you were sent after us. It could have been meant for this little meeting to take place, only for us to leave and cause havoc for you."

Something strange happens. Walter laughs at Jules's sensible reasoning. It is a soft but full and jolly chuckle.

"I thank you very much for your concern, Jules, but Oracles can only come from those who wield Blue Light."

The three of us are baffled into silence.

"I am sorry. What?" Jules snaps.

"Oracles require Blue Light," he repeats.

More time lapses in silence between us.

"You are unfamiliar with Blue Light Energy?"

"We have never heard of it," Josh answers.

Now, if Josh does not know anything about it, then Jules and I certainly do not.

"Oh, well, Blue Light Energy is in each of us," Walter says.

"It is in everyone with the best of intentions. Well, it can only be requested with the best of intentions. It takes a clean heart to use Blue Light, but once you avert yourself from a pure heart, it dissipates.

"Blue Light is an enhancer. It is the core of our training, as a matter of fact. Anyone can train until they are run-down and still not reach beyond a certain level of proficiency. We all have our limits. Blue Light, however, takes you beyond your limitations. Whatever you lack, Blue Light will make up for the deficit. If your *ability* is to *camouflage*, Blue Light could help you *camouflage* other people as well. Say your *ability* allows you to read the thoughts and emotions of others. Blue Light could help you read multiple people at the same time. It could even enable you to project your own thoughts and emotions to others. It is the supernatural ability to do what you cannot do on your own, basically."

I can hear the excitement and enthusiasm in Walter's voice. Quite frankly, it sparks my interest. Blue Light sounds amazing.

"What do you mean by 'requested'?" Josh asks.

"Well, that will come at a later time," Walter says dismissively as he looks at the wall opposite the three of us as though it conceals a powerful answer within its white boundaries.

Suddenly something occurs to me about this great and powerful force. "Wait. Walter."

His attention returns to me.

"You said that you cannot say where the Oracle came from. Is it that you cannot say or that you will not say?"

Josh and Jules look at me in confusion, wondering what I am talking about, but Walter's mouth slowly spreads into a wide smile that says he knows he has been caught and he is happy about it. He wants us to know.

"You know where the Oracle came from," I acknowledge.

Walter looks at me in silence for a moment. "And judging by the certainty in your conclusion, I gather that you know as well." He looks proud.

I am sure that Josh and Jules are confounded—Josh wondering why Walter lied, and Jules disturbed by the fact that he did. I do not look at them, though. I know why Walter claimed that he could not say where the Oracle came from. As Josh has said, Walter does not know us. He does not know who we are or what we are like. Perhaps he can trust that we will not exploit the Resistance, but how can he present something to us like the fact that this Blue Light Energy instructed him to come find us? For all that he knows, that could send us right out the door. It sounds crazy—preposterous—but it is true.

Besides, he obviously wants us to stay, out of the kindness of his heart, not out of some trickery or other form of conspiracy. He actually wants to help us, and ... I think that I am willing to let him.

"What are you talking about?" Josh asks.

"The Oracle was not conjured by some unknown entity," Walter explains. "It was from the Source of Blue Light itself. Blue Light is a very unique form of energy that no one can fully understand, but it contains complex abilities and properties, one being that it can serve as a sort of wise adviser, if you will."

"What?" Jules demands.

My mind flashes back to the Prophecy, and I wonder if Prophecies and Envisionments come from Blue Light as well.

"So," Josh cuts in, "you are saying that this ... force—that this ... energy ... is basically everything good and helpful that you can think of."

"Well," Walter responds, "we do not really know the extent of it, but it seems that way, yes."

A moment of silence lapses, and I break it with a question. "Where is it?"

"The Source?"

I nod.

"It varies. It has been in existence for as long as we can

trace—perhaps all the way back to the beginning of time, and maybe even before then. We do not know. It has been passed on from one location to another throughout the years. The Source's location may change constantly, but its power stretches everywhere continuously, no matter where the Source is."

"I am guessing that is how you have this powerful security system around these headquarters," Josh says. "The Blue Light Energy has boosted the *gifts* of some of the members here."

Walter nods.

"So ... in training ... we will be trained with this ... Blue Light as well?" I ask.

"Yes."

More time lapses in silence again. All of my questions and concerns have been addressed, but Josh and Jules seem to still be considering and digesting everything.

"So," Jules concludes, looking down at nothing, "we really are safe here."

Knowing Jules, she is not talking to anyone in particular. Impressively, Walter understands this and does not respond. He simply leaves time open, allowing for any further questions. None of us inquires any further, though.

"Well." Walter places his hands on the arms of his chair. "I think that it is about time the three of you got some rest. It has been a very long evening, and we have an early morning."

He pushes his chair back as he stands, and we all follow him to the narrow hallway. After this conversation, I suppose I can find a way to coexist with all these narrow passageways, though they vaguely remind me of the terrorizing maze back in the Fireburst Compound. As time goes on, I will grow accustomed to hallways as the passageways that they are, leading from one place to another, rather than viewing them as an endless maze of captivity and despair.

We walk through the hallway in silence, pass the narrow staircase, and come into the foyer with the chandelier, staircases, and numerous passageways again. Walter leads us up the nearest staircase and turns through the left archway. We follow him down a long corridor that stretches far away from us, encompassing at least twenty doors plus one that stands in the far wall, facing us.

The corridor walls are white with patterns of gold streaks, and the floor is carpeted with a pattern alternating between red and gold. Next to each door is a golden-brown slot holding slits of paper with words on them: *Rebirth, Intellect, Strength, Protection, Transformation* ... This mansion truly is massive.

We pass more doors until we are almost at the end of the

corridor, and Walter turns to face a brown door on the left that has no paper slip in the golden-brown slot next to it. He removes keys from his pocket, unlocks the door, pushes it open, and steps aside, gesturing for us to go in. I follow Jules into the room.

"This is not your permanent arrangement," Walter says as we enter, "but we did not have ample notice before reaching you three to prepare your rooms. I hope this will meet your satisfaction for tonight."

A bathroom is on our left with the lights off, and ahead of us is the bedroom, with beige walls, two beds facing the right wall, a nightstand, a lamp, and a desk. There is not a lot in here, but it is nice. Jules and I will have to share a bed.

"Thank you, Walter—for all of this," I hear behind me.

I turn around to see Josh shaking hands with Walter.

"You're welcome," Walter responds, elated. "I will come by in the morning to bring you three down to begin the day."

Walter leaves, and Josh closes the door behind him.

He takes a look in the bathroom as he passes it. "Well ..." he says, raising his arms and then dropping them at his sides.

"It is nice," I say.

The beds are on the left side of the room. They can easily accommodate two people. Between the two beds is the nightstand, with the lamp standing on it.

Jules purses her lips and nods in satisfaction as she looks up at the ceiling, continuing to examine the room. She strolls over to the nightstand.

"You two should share a bed," Josh says.

Jules and I both look at him with mockingly exasperated expressions.

"Really, Josh?" I say.

Josh puts his hands up in surrender. "All right, all right. I was only making sure."

Jules shakes her head and returns to examining our temporary quarters. While it is a lot of fun to look around the room at all of its contents, I am sure that I heard Walter say that we have to abide by the rules of this organization and that we have an early morning tomorrow.

"Well, I am going to go shower." I walk into the bathroom and turn on the light. The walls are white, of course, and the shower stands in the far corner on the right with sliding doors. The sink counter is on my left, underneath a large mirror spanning the wall. The toilet sits on the other side of the sink, near the far wall, which features a towel rack with some towels and washcloths hanging on it.

A white cubby stands between the shower and the bathroom door on my right. It almost reaches my height and obstructs the door from opening all the way. Its five sections are filled with fabrics of various colors that are neatly folded. The top section contains bright colors arranged into two piles. I take a piece of fabric and let it unfold in my hand. It is a long white T-shirt. I grab the next piece of fabric from the pile and let it unfold in my other hand. It is a pair of furry, light pink pants with a nice curving pattern down the legs.

They have left us clothes! I do not have to dress in this prison suit again after I shower! I feel so delighted. I never realized how much I loathe this jumpsuit until now. Too many things have been on my mind.

I look in the cubby and notice two more piles farther back. Examining other shelves, I discover sleepwear and daytime clothes. They have even left us undergarments, sweatshirts, washcloths, and a few other necessary items. The ceaseless gestures of kindness are refreshing after the turmoil that we have gone through. And by the looks of it, we can rid ourselves of these gray prison suits forever.

I distribute some of the clothes across my arms and step out to the bedroom to find Josh and Jules sitting on the beds, facing each other and talking. As I approach, they turn to face me. I raise my arms, putting the clothes on display. Josh and

Jules look stunned.

"We are saved!" I exclaim triumphantly.

"Oh, wow," Jules says.

I smile and go back into the bathroom. I neatly fold the clothes and return them to their respective piles. Everything we need and more is in this bathroom. There are toothbrushes in a holder next to a tube of toothpaste on the sink, a few bars of soap, mini bottles of body soap and shampoo, and a number of other things.

I brush my teeth and wash my face with the provided toiletries. It is amazingly refreshing to clean the inside of my mouth and my face. We have not had the opportunity to do so since we left home. The Firebursts do not provide luxurious—or even basic—necessities to their prisoners.

Washing my face now, though, I touch a tender spot on my jaw that I did not notice before. In the mirror, I see a soft bruise on the edge of my face. Other cuts and marks blemish my face as well, which did not feel sensitive until now as I stare at them in the mirror—remnants of being beaten in the Fireburst Compound. The torture was nowhere near as bad as it could have been, though. The beatings did not occur very often. However, I do not know how we could have survived if they did, because every session was brutal and progressively worse.

We were not there for too long, thankfully. We never saw the movement of the sun signifying day and night, but judging by the schedule of our rations, I would guess that we were captives there for about five to seven weeks. It is difficult to determine—especially considering the fact that I have no idea how long we were unconscious upon arriving there.

I slide the shower door open and turn on the shower. Standing on the soft blue mat, I feel delighted to unzip the prison suit, shedding the confining reminder of where we came from. I peel away the bondage and the imprisonment to release a new, free bird that is healing from a few bumps and bruises but is ready to fly away to a great land of promise.

I take a washcloth and leave the jumpsuit on the mat as I step into the shower, eager to freshen up. I suddenly feel so dirty—so bogged down with exhaustion and filth and the wear of the last few weeks—and I just need to wash it all off.

As I shower, I painfully discover more bruises and burns on my body that I was unaware of. There is a bruise that blotches my right thigh, one on my right shoulder, and one on my back. As soon as I come across the one on my back, I touch something else that strikes a sharp pain through me. It is far more sensitive to the touch than my other injuries and feels raw, sending my mind back to a distant memory.

I am in a torture chamber, where it is dimly lit and the air is moist. I am on the floor, curled up in a ball on the cold, wet stone, convulsing in pain while about five Firebursts stand around me in a circle. I am in too much pain and too exhausted to shield myself with my *field*—too broken to even feel it, or my muscles, or any other part of my body. All that I feel is pain. All that I know is pain, and it surrounds me.

They play around with me in combat, exhausting me until I have nothing left to fight back with. Then they torture me.

I lie here on the stone floor, trying to catch my breath, when another blow hits my back in a place that was already writhing in pain. A strangled cry escapes my lips with more air than I knew I had left in my lungs.

"WHERE IS IT?" they demand. "WHERE?"

They yell endlessly at me, and their booming voices echo ferociously throughout the chamber and back to my ears. There is no sense in asking what they are referring to. Whenever asked, they viciously retaliate, screaming, "You know exactly what we're talking about! Your division always spoke about it! You know about the Resistance! WHERE IS IT?"

They want to know about a resistance that is not even real, I think. *We only spoke about it at home. No one ever actually formed one.*

My thoughts do not matter, though. No one is listening to them. We are being punished with no hope of freedom because we do not know about a fictitious uprising. It is hopeless. It is pointless. There is no sense in trying to defend myself when they will only drain me in the end anyway. Eventually, I always end up in the same position: writhing on the floor in searing pain.

I am dwelling on my own hopelessness and misery—on the hopelessness and misery of all three of us—when a sudden burning sensation, hotter than anything I have ever felt before, ignites my back. A garbled scream explodes from my mouth and bubbles in my throat. The heat—the scorching heat—eats away at my flesh, and all that I know is the excruciating pain that spans across my back and sears through my insides to the front of my body.

I hear a sizzling sound above my head as the force from the attack subsides, leaving behind the pain like a permanent imprint on my back. I manage to look up to see sparks land on the stone above my head. I push past the agony to look back at the source of the attack and see the fire dissipating from the hand of a Fireburst.

They look at me with an expression of superiority, like I owe them something. No amount of screaming or excruciating pain will change anything. No sincere ignorance regarding their questions will make a difference. I can see it in their eyes, and I am afraid that I may give them the satisfaction of seeing me cry.

I return to the present. I am back to the nice, clean beige tiles and the warm water spewing from the showerhead. I am back to the newly found freedom and safety of this building. I need to cast those nightmares out of my mind. I can feel them subconsciously trying to eat away at the comfort that is developing inside me here.

I dispel the haunting memories of the Fireburst Compound with comforting memories of Walter and the Resistance. I think of the kind hospitality offered to us and the many supplies here. I think of Walter's kindness and the Resistance members' refusal to hurt any of us when all we did was hurt them. I think of Josh's *bolts* shocking people and Jules's *ice* cases entrapping people. I think of the man that I shoved into the air—I never found out what happened to him. I need to ensure that he is all right.

Tomorrow, I tell myself.

I finish showering and step onto the mat, feeling renewed. I dry myself with a towel from the rack and dress in the long white T-shirt, which falls down to my thighs, and the furry pink pants. I fold my gray suit and carry it out of the bathroom with me. Josh and Jules look at me with smiles all around, and I notice the cuts, bruises, and healing burns on them that were too much the norm to really notice before.

"Squeaky clean, Soph?" Jules asks.

I smirk. "Yes."

"I have to go to the bathroom really quickly," Josh says to Jules. "You are next to shower, though."

"That is really not necessa—"

"Uh-bup-bup-bup," he interjects, putting up his hand to silence her. "I mean it. You are going first."

Jules rolls her eyes and looks up hopelessly.

I cannot help but smile at them.

Josh passes me and walks into the bathroom. I walk between

the beds and sigh in satisfaction as I settle on the one across from Jules, where Josh was sitting. It is so soft and welcomingly succumbs to my weight. It briefly reminds me of the silver substance in the passageway that we followed Walter through.

I feel exhaustion weigh me down as I examine the bed. I find myself eyeing the fluffy white pillows that are stacked in two layers, side by side, against the headboard. I pull the sheets back, ready to forsake all worries in a land of nothingness.

"Hey," Jules calls. "Your place is here with me." She pats the other side of the bed that she is sitting on. "Josh has to sleep somewhere."

"Well," I say, smiling with anticipation as I settle underneath the sheets. "Then I guess you will have to sleep in this bed next to me, and Josh can sleep in that bed … because I am sleeping here."

Jules smiles and shakes her head at me.

"At least for a few minutes, I would like to stretch out with no restraints."

Jules laughs softly to herself and stretches out on the other bed as I get comfortable in mine. I think that I am asleep before my eyes even close.

Jules might have sighed and said something along the lines of, "This place seems really great."

I agree, of course. And there are so many things to discuss, but I think all that manages to come out is a moan.

Chapter 7

THE SOUND OF HOLLOW taps makes my eyes shoot open before I am even aware that I am awake. I lie there, listening for the sound, but there is complete silence. Then I hear three knocks at the door.

"Jules? Josh? Sophie? It is time to wake up. Breakfast will be downstairs momentarily!" It is Walter. Three more polite knocks sound at the door.

"All right, we will be down there in a minute!" I call back to him. I have no idea where breakfast will be downstairs, but I am sure that we can figure it out.

There is no response. I lay my head back down on the pillow, feeling slightly discombobulated. The sleep was so good. It was the first peaceful rest that we have had in a long time.

Recent sleep has consisted of scarce naps between spasms of pain, torture, and nightmares. This sleep had none of those things.

I do not want to fall back to sleep, though, so I make a concerted effort to blink several times at the daylight seeping in through the closed blinds of a window on the opposite side of the other bed, trying to wake myself up. I was too exhausted to notice that window last night.

My body does not want to move. I carefully flex my *field* in my hands, not wanting to disturb Jules beside me. However, strangely enough, there is no one next to me in this bed. I am lying in the center of the two stacks of pillows and am stretched out over the bed. Clearly, I was very drained.

I feel like I am taking up too much room, so I shift to one side and face the other bed, wondering if Josh and Jules decided to share it for some reason. Perhaps I took up too much space in this bed, but no, there is only one body under those sheets, which slowly rises and falls with slow, soft breaths. I look around the room and do not see Jules.

"Josh! Josh!" I call in a whisper, not wanting to alarm him.

Josh reluctantly sits up and turns around to look at me. Only, it is not Josh.

"Jules?"

Her hair is everywhere from sleeping roughly, and her eyes are squinted after just waking up. I wonder if I look the same way.

She yawns with one hand over her mouth and stretches with the other. "Good morning."

"Where is Josh?"

Her stretch and yawn cut off abruptly. "Oh. Um ..." She looks around bashfully. Then she points to the floor in between us.

I crawl to the edge of the bed and look down. Josh is sleeping on the floor with a blanket. I am genuinely confused.

"Wait a minute," I say to her. "I thought that you and I were supposed to share a bed, and he was supposed to sleep in that one."

"Well," she says, waving her hand dismissively, "he just told me to take the bed and insisted on sleeping on the floor."

This sounds odd considering the fact that this was the first opportunity for a really nice sleep that we have had in a long time. Surely, he could not have slept as well on the floor as he would have in the bed, but I do not pursue it.

"All right. Well, Walter just stopped by. We have to go downstairs for breakfast."

Jules lets off a bigger, dramatic yawn. "Well, I guess we better wake him," she says, gesturing to Josh.

I nod and reach down to wake him up, but blue *ice* crawls over his body where I was about to touch him. My hand draws back in surprise before I realize that it is just Jules. I look up at her reproachfully and see her teasing smirk. She used to wake me up like this on occasion when we would sleep together at home. I cannot help but smile with anticipation to see someone else deal with it while I simply watch on the sidelines.

The *ice* reaches Josh's neck and slides down his back under his T-shirt. Not even a full second passes before he is on his feet, yelping and panicking, reaching for the cold sting that slithers down his back.

Jules and I erupt with laughter, and it feels so good. The *ice* falls out of Josh's shirt, and he starts laughing too. It has been a long time since we last laughed—since we last smiled. It has been a long time since we were even a ghost resemblance of ourselves.

Josh recovers from his laughter. "Ha ha ha. Very funny, girls."

Jules and I slow our laughter.

"I do not know, Josh. I thought it was pretty hysterical, to say the least," Jules teases.

Josh just shakes his head, but then I remember that we need

to leave the room. "Oh, Josh. We need to go downstairs." Dramatically I add, "Breakfast is being served."

"Well, why did you not say so earlier?"

He rushes into the bathroom. In two seconds, he comes back out with a toothbrush in his mouth to pick up the *ice* on the floor that fell down his shirt. He walks back into the bathroom to dispose of it, and I remember what Jules told me this morning.

"Hey, Josh!" I call.

He returns from the bathroom, still brushing his teeth.

"Why did you insist on sleeping on the floor? Jules and I could have shared a bed."

Josh freezes and looks at me blankly before he takes the toothbrush out of his mouth. "Well, when I came out from the shower last night, I found that you two had taken over both of the beds, so I had no choice," he says cheerily around a mouthful of toothpaste. He inserts the toothbrush back in his mouth and continues brushing.

I look at Jules pointedly. "Jules!"

She shrugs with innocently raised hands, mouthing confused babbles as though she has no idea what Josh is talking about.

"Did I miss something?" Josh asks, looking back and forth

between us.

"Well," I say, "little Ms. Innocence over here told me that you insisted on sleeping on the floor."

She gasps and fakes an appalled expression. "What? Me?" she asks mockingly.

I shake my head as we all laugh and disperse to prepare for the day. In a few minutes, we manage to quickly take turns in the bathroom, get dressed, and make our beds. While getting ready, I remember the vow that I made to myself last night about the man who I shoved yesterday. I will have to remember to ask Walter when I see him at breakfast … maybe.

Just as we are ready to go downstairs, three knocks come at the door. "Are you three ready to come downstairs?" It is Walter again.

Josh goes to open the door while Jules and I trail behind him. "We are ready," he says.

"Excellent!" Walter peeks over Josh's shoulder at me and Jules. "Good morning, ladies."

"Good morning," we say.

"If you three would please follow me," Walter says, and he begins walking down the hallway to the stairs.

I was correct about becoming accustomed to the corridors here. Already they do not feel as threatening as they did yesterday.

"Breakfast can be a little busy, but I think that you three will like it," he says as we walk down the corridor. "After breakfast is when the fun really begins."

I wonder what he means by "fun." Suddenly I am exceptionally eager to find out, but of course, I will have to wait.

Initially, my intention was to ask Walter about the man from yesterday at breakfast, but this seems to be as good a time as any to ask him. I step up around Josh so that I am beside Walter.

"Walter, there was a man that I ... might have hurt yesterday. I shoved him pretty hard. Do you know of him ... if he is all right?" I figure that it may be a good idea to leave out the detail of exactly how hard I pushed him.

Walter looks ahead. "Yes. He is fine."

I sigh in relief, releasing a burden that I did not even realize weighed so heavily on my chest.

"As well as those who fell into the forest," he adds.

I freeze. "What?" escapes my lips of its own accord, but his addendum is only logical. Just last night, Walter confirmed that the forest by the hedge is in fact dangerous. And I shoved several people into it. Based on how Walter described that forest, shoving people in there was even worse than what I did to the man who I shoved into the air.

Walter looks a little concerned about me. The confusion and guilt in my heart must be visible on my face. "You ... pushed some people into the forest last night," he says hesitantly.

I can tell that if he had known that I was not even considering that dangerous act, he would not have mentioned it. He knows that I already have regrets about hurting these people, and he does not want to add to them. Still, I am glad that he brought it to my attention. I should know—not for self-pity reasons, but I should know the extent of the damage that I have done and the consequences thereof. That is the way of a Conqueror.

"I am so sorry," I say. "I did not realize—I mean, I should have—"

Walter lets out a soft chuckle. "It is okay, Sophie. Don't worry about it. They are all fine."

I nod as we turn to descend the huge staircase, and I let go of the guilt and sorrow, knowing that it cannot and will not change anything.

"So, what is for breakfast?" Josh asks at the foot of the stairs. He has been enthusiastic about the idea of food all morning. As soon as I mentioned it earlier, he sped to get ready to leave the room. Now he is inquiring about it when we cannot be more than five minutes away from it.

"Well, let me see ..." Walter begins to count the options on his fingers. "We have French toast, pancakes, waffles, scrambled eggs, sausages, grits, and fruit salad. Plus some orange juice, tea, coffee, and water."

I salivate and hear Josh's stomach growl.

"It sounds delicious," Jules says.

"Oh, I think it is," Walter replies as we turn left, crossing the foyer, to enter the lounge area. The space is just as tall and immense as the foyer, and it is lavished with regal textures. Across the room from us, ornate red-and-brown drapes cascade over three massive windows that stretch along the tall wall. Two tall bookcases extend along the wall between the windows and are equipped with an endless array of books. There are so many.

We turn left again and walk along the side of the room on a narrow, ornate rug with beautiful red-and-brown designs. It serves as a pathway through the room. A few luxurious reclining chairs sit dispersed throughout the space, and a little wooden coffee table with a glass top stands right in front of a red couch that faces this side of the room. Next to the couch is a lamp on an end table, and two plush red armchairs sit on either side of the table, facing each other. Furniture, rugs, colors, and patterns surround us in regality, and I finally have the opportunity to admire the peculiar beauty of this mansion.

"Wow, Walter," I say. "This is truly beautiful."

"Thank you. You do not see these things very often, do you?"

"Not at all," Jules says.

Following the carpet through the room, we approach double doors that are already open to a fairly large tan room. Having been preoccupied with admiring the lounge area, I only now begin to notice the clatter and the delectable smell that pours out from the tan room in front of us. We step into the room and to what almost resembles chaos.

A long mahogany table stretches to our right through the center of the rectangular room, with food, eating utensils, and at least twenty people. A tall hutch stands against the wall that we just entered through, about midway along the table. White cabinetry extends on our left to the nearby corner, framing yet another doorway in the left side of the room, and continues on the other side of the doorway. A few decorative pictures hang on the walls all around the room, and to our right, a plant on a stand sits in one corner while a stand holds a statue in the other.

Through the doorway on our left is what appears to be a kitchen. I see another set of doors that leads from the kitchen to another room, which must be perpendicular to this one. I believe that I hear clatter coming from there, and I think that I see another table, which probably also accommodates a lot of people.

"Good morning, everyone!" Walter calls out.

An outcry of responsive greetings meets Walter from the three rooms with bright smiles all around.

"Everyone, this is Jules, Sophie, and Josh." He gestures to each of us. "Make them welcome. They are our new family, and ... try not to chase them away," he says, feigning desperation.

The room rumbles with low chuckles, and a nervous smile tugs at my lips.

There are so many people here. There are definitely more members than we saw last night—some of which we may have hurt. This last consideration makes me feel a little uncomfortable, but I decide to push past it.

There are a few seats available toward the far end of the table, and Walter gestures for us to have a seat.

"You three can sit over there and enjoy your breakfast," he says. "I will just be checking on a few things in the kitchen and in the other dining room."

Walter steps through the left doorway, and we walk along the table to fend for ourselves. The room is full of chatter, with smiles and different dialects as people ask for the syrup to be passed and make jokes, telling stories about training and other members' embarrassing moments. Apparently, someone named John pushed his *ability* too hard and caused a little disturbance in some mud, which exploded and splattered everywhere—including on his pants, which caused some confusion when he came out of training.

The three of us find two seats together that are practically at the end of the table and one seat across from them. Josh has me and Jules sit together while he goes around the table and sits on the other side. The seats already have plates and utensils set up before them.

I sit next to a male with short dark brown hair, wearing a black T-shirt and gray sweatpants, who glances at me and smiles warmly. I smile back. Jules is next to a woman. Josh sits between a woman with a mature face and long black hair and a thick man with short brown hair that softly flips up at the front. The people that we sit among are already involved in separate conversations, split by the small chasm of empty chairs we have just filled. Interestingly enough, our presence seems to draw them together.

"Well, would you look who it is!" the male across the table says, breaking away from his conversation with people on the other side of Jules to look at us. He rests one arm on the table, leaning toward us with fascinated eyes. "The hit-and-run pack."

"Oh, ease up, John," the male next to me says.

So, this is John, I think. It is beneficial to have ears.

John leans back in his seat, withdrawing his arm with a joking smile on his face.

"I'm David," the male next to me says. He offers his hand to me, and I shake it.

"Sophie," I say. "And this is Jules." I point to her. He nods in her direction. "And Josh," I conclude, tilting my head across the table.

"Pleasure to meet you all," David says.

"Nice to meet you, David," Josh says.

"Indeed," Jules says over me. "It is nice to meet someone with some manners." She glances mischievously at John.

"Ooh."

David and John laugh while John has his hands up in surrender.

Josh is looking down at the food he has so quickly gathered on his plate, but I can see that he is laughing too. Who cannot laugh at Jules and her comical outspoken tendencies?

"Watch out, John." The woman next to Josh smiles at Jules

while holding a piece of waffle on a fork halfway to her mouth. "This one's got a mouth on her."

"Yeah, I know," he says. "It looks like I've got some competition."

The woman and David start laughing.

I confidently reach for a waffle on a silver platter to collect on my plate. "It seems odd that he has so much mouth, considering the fact that he came out of a training session looking like he had an accident," I say.

I am so happy that I listen, because the conversation goes completely silent for a moment. The woman next to Josh has wide, astonished eyes, and I hear nothing from David until he makes a spitting sound, bursting out in hysterical laughter. The woman next to Josh immediately laughs too. Even the woman on the other side of Jules is laughing. Jules just smiles confidently, and Josh looks up from his food, impressed by me. His eyes show his curiosity, and he is not the only one.

"How do you know about that?" John demands.

I innocently crease my eyebrows as I reach for the syrup that sits between me and David and pour it on my waffle. "What ever do you mean, brownnoser?"

As I cut into my waffle, I can feel my mouth salivating for real food, not just rations served behind bars.

The woman and David are still laughing, and John sits back, folding his arms in wonderment. I can imagine his thoughts: *Did she hear about it from someone? Can she read people's thoughts?*

I feel pleased with myself as I stare him down and plop a scrumptious piece of syrup-saturated waffle into my mouth.

"Thank you very much, Sophie," the woman next to Josh says, regaining her composure. "I'm sorry. Where are my manners? I'm Margaret."

"Mmm," I acknowledge around a mouthful of food. I put a hand over my mouth. "Hi, Margaret."

Jules and Josh greet her as well.

"You have to forgive John," David says. "I think he still has a bit of a grudge against you."

"Oh?" I am genuinely confused, seeing as we have never met before.

David leans over to me and says, just loud enough for John to overhear and look pointedly back at him, "John's not used to being thrown around like a rag doll."

At first, I think that David is referring to how Jules and I tag-teamed against him, but seeing John's reaction makes me realize it is something more than that. Then it occurs to me. The person that I shoved into the air last night ... it was John.

I open my mouth, about to apologize, but he interrupts me. "No need for your apologies now. My bruises are all patched up enough by your kind words, thank you very much."

Margaret rolls her eyes and sends a sympathetic look in my direction.

"John is a little dramatic, you may come to find," David says.

"Oh, I have noticed," Jules says.

John pretends to be insulted, placing a hand over his chest and looking around defensively. "I am not."

Josh smirks to himself as he eats his pancakes, too preoccupied to say anything.

"Believe it or not, that was a pretty high trajectory," John says in his defense.

"Oh, please, John. You could probably fall from thirty feet in the air and land without a scratch," Margaret replies, pointedly looking across Josh at him. She looks back at me. "John can manipulate the earth enough that he can pass right through it. He can just ... sink down and come back up without a particle of dirt on him."

"Wow, that must come in handy," I say.

"No kidding," comments Jules.

"Exactly," Margaret responds. "So again I point out, no big deal."

"Hey," John protests, "it is a very big deal."

Margaret throws her hands up in exasperation.

"What if I had an off day? What if I couldn't manipulate land, huh?"

Margaret shakes her head in annoyance as he rants.

I honestly find it quite amusing that someone can talk so much.

Jules is giggling next to me, amused herself.

"Don't mind him," Margaret says to me.

"He'll get over his little hissy fit," David says. "He always does."

We all laugh again. More and more laughter floods this place, and I find myself feeling so grateful that we are here. We only arrived last night, and already we have come across people that we like—at least, that I like. And judging by the lack of nauseated expressions furtively exchanged between the three of us, I gather that Josh and Jules like them too.

"So, are you guys going to train with us?" David asks.

"Yes. We start the same schedule as everyone else today," Jules says.

"Great," John says enthusiastically. "We'll get to see what you guys are really capable of."

Margaret jabs a thumb in John's direction, looking at David

in disbelief.

David smiles and responds with a helpless shrug.

We go through breakfast talking about our impression of the building and John's unique personality. Afterward, we take all of our dishes into the rectangular kitchen, which is filled with cabinetry, except for the wall on our left, the one with the other doorway. A long kitchen island with a counter-top made of blue pearl granite stretches across the center of the room. Beyond the island is a long blue pearl granite counter that spans across the wall. Underneath the counter, two large ovens are set in the cabinetry on opposite ends. Closer to the center are two dishwashers, and then side by side are two sinks in the center of the countertop. Two more ovens sit at eye level in the wall we just entered through and the far wall opposite us. The kitchen is neat and organized, and it is fit to cater for a lot of people.

A number of people file into the kitchen and around the island to put away their dishes. They quickly rinse and wipe them in the sink before putting them in the farthest dishwash-er.

"We pack all the dishes into one dishwasher before we start putting dishes in the other," Margaret explains to us.

About eight people put their dishes away before it is our

turn. Margaret moves to the sink first. She wipes down her dishes with a soapy sponge and puts them in the left dishwasher, which is nearly full. She holds her hand out, offering to take my things for me. I hand her my tableware with a grateful "Thank you," and she wipes them down. There is no more room for plates in the dishwasher, but there is room for silverware and my cup in the top tray. When she puts the cup and silverware into the dishwasher, she closes it and waves her free hand at us, telling us to move back.

We take a few steps back, past the other dishwasher. She opens it and puts my plate in there. She takes Josh's and Jules's tableware as well. David and John try to get the same treatment by offering Margaret their things.

"Oh, no, you don't," she says. "I'm not a maid. It's their first time, so I was just being nice and showing them the ropes around here. You two, on the other hand"—she points an accusatory finger at them—"are not new." She grabs the sponge and cheerily hands it to them. "Here you go. Your reward for your service to the Resistance."

John takes it begrudgingly, and Margaret strides through all of us triumphantly.

I glance at Josh with a look of hilarity on my face.

"I know," he mouths.

Josh, Jules, and I make our way through David and John so that we are not in their way. As they put their dishes away, four more people come in from the second dining room. They travel around the island and wait a respectful few feet behind John and David.

Meanwhile, Walter appears in the doorway from the second dining room. "Did everyone enjoy their breakfast?"

Everyone says yes and thanks him.

I am surprised. "You cooked all of this food?"

"Goodness, no," he says. "I cooked some of it but not alone. Some people here are very fast, so they are a great help when it comes to things like cooking for forty-eight people—well, forty-nine including myself."

I wonder if the "fast" people that he refers to are simply fast workers or if they have a *fast ability*.

"So." Walter claps and rubs his hands together. "Have you three built up some energy?"

I am taken aback by his peculiar question. Margaret, David, and John exchange knowing expressions with one another. Margaret turns to face us, purposefully smiling. I cannot help but genuinely wonder what we are in for.

"Yes," Josh says hesitantly.

Walter smiles. "Good. Then let's get going."

He turns around to walk back into the second dining room, and the six of us follow. This room is also rectangular and stretches out in front of us. Traveling through it, along the mahogany dining table and chairs, I see that this room looks exactly like the one that we ate in. The only differences are the pictures and the positions of the doors. In the first room, the doors are practically next to each other while these doors are on opposite ends of the room.

"Dare I ask what we are getting into?" I ask Margaret.

All she says is "You'll see."

Chapter 8

WALTER OPENS THE DOOR at the end of the dining room, and we follow him into the foyer, stepping out from underneath one of the staircases. Now I know where four of these multiple passageways lead, and something tells me that I am about to discover the destination of another.

Walter walks to the wall between the two staircases that tower above us, underneath the balcony. This wall and the ones underneath the staircases are a dark ruby with curving scarlet patterns that resemble those in the corridor upstairs. Walter touches a button in the wall that I cannot see, and a piece slides back and into a slot to the right, revealing a dark open doorway.

Walter steps in and does something to the right, just inside the doorway. Perhaps there is a switch or another button.

Suddenly a burst of flame ignites a torch on the wall a couple of feet ahead of him. As he approaches it and removes it from the medieval sconce, I notice that this open doorway is an entrance to a narrow stone staircase that spirals downward, like the one that Josh, Jules, and I descended in the old mansion by the hedge.

The staircase is ancient and made of rough stone. More dim, dancing flickers of orange light suddenly appear farther down the staircase. More torches must have ignited. The staircase's ancient appearance seems oddly misplaced in this lavish, furnished mansion where everything seems to be bright and polished.

Torch in hand, Walter waves for us to follow him. We all progress down the shallow, spiraling stone steps. The staircase is small, so we have to proceed in single file, like we did in the white corridor leading to Walter's office. The spirals are also close together, leaving only a couple of feet free above our heads. Our footsteps echo against the stone and reverberate in my ears in an unmelodic procession that melds together into a blur of noise.

Every few steps, we pass another torch on the wall, further illuminating the way. Naturally, I start to feel my *field* in my palms. I may feel safe in this mansion with these people, but this place does not make me feel like I am in the mansion. It is too old, too dark, and it reminds me too much of the life on the run that we just came from.

I try to relax with deep, steady breaths and with the remembrance that these are the same people that I feel safe with, that I was laughing with, that I can trust. One more torch comes into view before I see the base of the staircase.

Lights automatically turn on in the open space beyond the steps. Walter must be low enough to have turned them on, or his movements were enough to activate them.

He reaches the floor of our destination just before I do. We stand in a corner of a large space that reaches about twenty feet in height and stretches about twenty by fifty yards to our right.

Walter places his torch in an empty sconce on the wall, which I suppose is there specifically for the purpose of commuting back and forth with a lit torch. I follow him along the shorter wall of the rectangular space to the far corner. We wait as everyone else files in. I did not realize how many people followed us down here. It is not just me, Jules, Josh, Margaret, David, and John. About thirty other people file in as well and line up against the wall.

"Is that everyone?" Walter asks no one in particular.

Everyone looks at the staircase to see if anyone else is coming in. No one walks down.

"Hmm ... well, let's begin." He walks out a few yards into the space and turns to face our assembled line. "As you all know, we have new guests here. They are very nice individuals, and I expect you to continue to treat them with the utmost kindness." He seems to look particularly in the direction of Margaret, David, and John when he adds approvingly, "As you have been, I am sure."

He speaks with the same authoritative voice that I remember hearing by the hedge. It is the voice that made everyone come to a halt—even me.

"Today will be the same as any other, and our new guests will participate just as most of you did when you first came here. To get them a little acclimated to how we do things around here—"

He is interrupted as a few more people come down the stairs and join the rest of us against the wall.

"Wonderful for you all to join us," he says, and he continues as if there had been no interruption. "I will begin with a short review of the fundamental rules, and we will have a couple of rounds before they duel."

I am shocked by the word "duel," wondering what he means. Although, chances are, I already know exactly what he means: we must fight one another.

"When I say, you withdraw immediately. You do not push yourself beyond your limits, but you do try. You do not ridicule or mock one another, and you keep in mind that this is a training session—nothing more, nothing less. So the purpose is to build you and your teammates up, not to tear you down—mentally, physically, or in any other way. Blue Light is an optional weapon, but it is only to be used when no alternative presents itself. The same goes for any other tactic or resource besides your *ability*. And of course, you do not go for the kill—not that I expect any of you to do so, but it is a rule nonetheless. Be very careful, for the sake of yourselves and others. While you are facing your opponent, be mindful that there are bystanders over here. So be careful in emitting stray strikes."

I suppose nothing outside of *abilities* is really utilized down here in order to hone our *abilities*. However, considering the regulations that Walter mentioned, I wonder just how intense this training session becomes. Then again, if these people really are more trained than Josh, Jules, and I are, then I cannot imagine that it is anything less than intense.

Walter signals someone from the line to come forward. I cannot see who he signals until they take a few steps away from the group. A young male in green sweatpants and a green shirt, lean and no taller than I am, walks to Walter's side and faces the line of people while Walter scans for an opponent. He signals someone else, and a woman in fitted pants and a tight black tank top steps forward. She looks bold and confident, with her head held high as if to proclaim, *I am ready for this.* She walks to Walter's other side.

"These are our first two contestants today. Remember everything you have learned," he says, "and use your heads."

He steps away from them, rejoining the line against the wall, while the boy and the woman walk farther into the room. Moments that stretch into endless minutes pass as they go about three-quarters of the way across the space. Eventually, they stop walking and face one another from opposite sides of the area.

All is still for a moment. Not a single motion is visible. Not a single sound is audible. Then a flash of orange appears from the woman's side, and the boy leaps out of the way, just fast enough to avoid being hit. Almost before I have registered the attack, the woman swings her arm, throwing another orange flash of *light* in the blink of an eye and reminding me of Josh's rapid attacks last night as we attempted to flee from these people.

The boy swipes his arm across his face, and I worry, doubtful that bare skin can stand against whatever *ability* this woman has, until I notice something trailing in the path of the boy's arm. Unexpectedly, the orange *light* is deflected and hits the ceiling.

Again, the woman throws *light*, and the boy swipes his arm just as fast, leaving a momentary wake of something white and glimmering that disappears too quickly for me to see. It knocks the woman's *light* strike up to the ceiling again. They combat back and forth like this for several more quick, jerky movements, until the boy launches an object formed by his *ability* at the woman.

Now the manifestation of the boy's *ability* exists long enough for me to see what it is. He has created a huge vertical sheet of strong, thick *glass* that almost reaches the ceiling, and he pushes it toward the woman, trapping her behind it. The couple of orange *light* slashes she throws at it only deflect back in her direction, so she stops and retreats from the encroaching wall of *glass*, as though it is a death sentence.

Then she juts her hands out to create two thin, horizontal sheets of the orange *light*, one along the ceiling and the other on the floor, and she slides them against the upper and lower borders of the *glass*. There appears to be hardly any resistance as she brings her hands together to squeeze the *light* through the *glass*, turning it into powder that falls like a curtain between her and the boy.

As the *glass* transforms into powder, the boy shoots a long stake of *glass* at her, which she quickly counters with a flash of *light* from her hand, instantly turning it into powder. She releases her other hand as the remnant of the thick, powdery curtain falls to the ground and as another shard of *glass* comes her way. Another flash of *light* shatters the stake into powder, which falls right at her feet.

The woman strides swiftly toward the boy, who throws more stakes faster. One after another, the woman throws *light* flashes just as quickly as the boy attacks her. The *light* works through the *glass* faster than it did before, appearing to eat away at the stakes before even reaching them and instantaneously making them fall to the ground as powder. Two stakes go down—three—five. Right arm—left arm—right—left—right—left. The reflexes on both ends are impeccable. The woman reaches the boy and throws *light* all around him, beginning to engulf him in an orange bubble, and the boy's hands whip up by his head—

"Time!" Walter calls.

The boy and the woman freeze in their tracks, and immediately the *light* ball disappears and the boy drops his hands. They return to the line, talking, laughing, and playfully nudging one another. They are making fun of the intense training. Mixing training and buoyancy like this is an unexpected concept for me, but it is interesting. Though the training session is trying and severe, the boy and the woman are still united—a team—a unit of good friendship. We had something like this at home, but it did not include this level of banter and good spirits.

Walter examines our line, searching for the next two people to call forth as the previous two contestants return. "Roger and ... Tony." Walter returns to the line as the two males step forward and pass the returning contestants on their way to their positions for combat.

"You're going down, Roger!" Tony calls across the space.

"Not before you, Tony!" Roger calls back.

They go back and forth with trash talk until they reach their destinations, where the boy and the woman previously stood.

Again, there is a moment of stillness, only this moment is shorter. With no warning at all, Tony launches a continuous tunnel of *water* at Roger. Roger throws up his arm to deflect it with a plate of *steel*, and a loud crash is audible upon impact. Holding the *steel* shield against the battering tunnel of *water*,

Roger forms a thick strap of *steel* around his arm to hold the plate in place.

The *water* tunnel stops, and Roger takes advantage of the pause to create a flat *steel* circle just above the ground with his free hand. Tony squirts a short tunnel of *water* at Roger, but Roger hops onto the *steel* disk before it hits him. The fact that the *water* travels across the expansive space says that there is substantial force behind it, but the audible sound it makes when it hits the wall behind Roger—and how far the *water* splatters—makes it clear just how dangerous Tony's attacks are. Just that little squirt alone sounds like a crashing tidal wave.

More *water* attacks come his way, but Roger flies on the *steel* plate around the area, dodging them. With the shield still in tow, Roger does a few flips and tricks to dodge the powerful *water* spurts until he approaches Tony.

He slows, but Tony launches another spurt of *water* at him. Roger flips over Tony toward us and speeds away, in our direction. Tony launches another *water* attack at Roger, and I think that Roger is going to be hit, because he is facing away from Tony and seems to wait too long to respond.

To my surprise, Roger pivots around just in time to throw a band of *steel* right through the tunnel of *water*, splitting the tunnel in two so that he is not hit, and fastens the piece of *steel* around Tony's hand so that he cannot spout *water* from it. Tony looks down at his hand in surprise, and Roger uses the pause to his advantage as he circles back around and throws a band around Tony's other hand and then another around Tony's head to cover his mouth. I wonder if Tony can control *water* with his mouth as well.

Roger hovers over his original position across the duel space from Tony and throws a long band of *steel* around Tony's left wrist, pulls it to his other wrist, and binds them together. Tony looks helplessly constrained by *steel*.

Roger hops off his *steel* disk to the ground a couple of feet below but winds up hopping into a large pool of *water* that suddenly appears around him, engulfing him and his *steel* disk and sending him into a seemingly uncontrollable frenzy of twists and twirls. There are no visible walls containing the swirling *water*, yet it remains within boundaries under Tony's command as he swings his bound hands in quick, barely perceptible circles in front of him to Roger's demise.

Tony makes a quick jerk of his hands to remove the *steel* disk from the pool, quickly followed by the *steel* shield that was securely attached to Roger's hand. The *water* continues to toy with Roger, pushing him down to the bottom and swirling and twirling him around so much and so fast that it confuses my eyes. It is a good thing that Tony removed those *steel* items, or Roger could be seriously injured in this predicament.

"Time!" Walter calls.

The *water* immediately slows and falls gently to the floor, carefully laying Roger down, but the *steel* constraints around Tony's hands and head remain. Roger lies on the floor on his stomach, coughing as he raises himself on his hands and pushes back into a sitting position. With a lazy—or weak—hand, Roger waves in Tony's direction and makes all the *steel* restraints disappear. Tony massages his wrists and his mouth as he crosses the space between himself and Roger, who is still sitting on the ground, sputtering and coughing. Tony extends a hand to him. Roger takes it with a hollow clap, and Tony pulls him to his feet.

As they walk back here, Roger gives Tony a lighthearted punch to the shoulder, and I hear him say, "That's for trying to drown me."

They laugh, only for Roger to break into another fit of coughs.

There is a delay before Walter comes forward from the line again. He was probably making sure that Roger was all right before continuing.

"John and Josh."

I suppress the smirk that rises in me, because this is so ironic—or intentional. John, who we just had breakfast with but who also refers to us as the "hit-and-run pack." His little grudge is really only toward me for shoving him into the air, but I still feel slightly uneasy about Josh fighting him. Nonetheless, Josh can take care of himself—even if these people seem to be very highly trained. He is a fast learner, at least. He should be fine.

Walter rejoins the line as Josh and John walk forward and pass Roger and Tony, who calmly return to the group. Roger is still drenched.

"Be careful of the wet spot!" Walter calls to Josh and John. The place where Tony released Roger is darker than the rest of the ground. It is still just as drenched as Roger is.

Josh looks back at Walter and nods while John extends a fist toward Walter with a thumb pointing up in the air. They continue their stroll to the duel area.

"And take it easy! This is Josh's first time, John!" Walter calls.

"Try not to have an accident this time, all right, John?" Josh calls over the space between them as they split to reach their starting positions. Josh pats the air in John's direction as though to comfort him. "You do not have to be intimidated by me."

John lets out a short burst of laughter. "You won't be joking around like that once I'm through with you."

Uneasiness returns to me.

They take their places: Josh on the left side and John on the right. There are a few moments of stillness, as usual. The first movement is Josh looking down around his feet. He jerks his head back and forth, examining the ground. I wonder what he is doing, but then I realize that he is getting shorter. No, he is not becoming shorter. He is sinking. He is standing right where Roger was, so the ground already has moisture in it, which must make it easy for John to manipulate the mud to his advantage.

Josh is sinking quickly and needs to formulate a plan immediately. He stretches his hands at his sides and strikes the ground with electric *bolts*, drying the ground after Tony's water stunt, I suppose. After a few seconds, he stops sinking. Even if the ground is dry, though, John could still sink him, from what we have heard about his *ability*.

Sure enough, the ground begins to cave in at Josh's feet. Josh thrusts his hands into the ground. It must still be a little muddy. Almost immediately, he is spewed out of a sudden bubbly eruption of mud. He must have created enough forceful bubbles to expel himself from the ground. I smile in triumph. It takes someone like Josh to think of something so clever.

Josh lands a few feet away from John on his stomach. A *bolt* flies from Josh, but John blocks it with a pillar of *dirt* that he instantly erects from the ground. Josh shoots another one at John at a different angle, but another pillar blocks it. Josh quickly rolls across the ground in our direction, shooting *bolts* at John, but John swiftly erects a wall of earthen pillars that blocks each *bolt*.

Unsuccessful at circumventing the protective wall, Josh suddenly jumps to his feet and *bolts* at a gap in it. John perfects the wall just in time, sealing off every opportunity of entry, before Josh's *bolt* goes through it. Josh stands ready with his knees bent and hands open, waiting for John to expose himself with another attack.

A flash of brown randomly shoots in front of Josh's face from the right, barely missing his head. His gaze follows the trajectory of the projectile to the ground in surprise. As soon as it lands a foot to his left, another batch of *dirt* spews out from the right wall. Josh promptly ducks, practically falling to the ground, and barely misses the blow. John must have left a tiny hole in his protective wall to see through.

Two more batches fly at Josh from the left wall, one above the other, but Josh is only ready for one. He blocks the one aimed at his head with crossed arms, but he misses the lower projectile, which hits him in the chest and knocks him to the ground.

John's earthen wall is suddenly swiped away, and he purposefully strides toward Josh. Josh quickly recovers with spurts of *bolts* aimed at his opponent from his inconvenient position on the ground. John effortlessly produces incredibly dense gatherings of *dirt* that somehow manage to absorb each *bolt* in midair. The *dirt* particles do not even come from John's hands but appear to form out of thin air as John nears Josh. Josh *bolts* with one hand, but a gathering of *dirt* appears to absorb it. Josh shoots with the other, and another *dirt* cloud consumes it.

As a *dirt* cloud absorbs yet another incoming *bolt*, John forms another gathering of *dirt* with his hand and launches it at Josh. Josh is left dumbfounded as it swarms around him and as John stands over him, focusing the energy of the massive swarm on Josh. I cannot even see Josh through the thick *dirt* swarm. I find myself feeling uncomfortable. Josh is better than this. He is the best fighter out of the three of us, and I do not know how John is managing to use his *ability* in such an advanced way to conquer Josh's.

Just when the battle seems to be over for Josh, a blinking yellow light appears in the midst of the swarm, like lightning in a thunderstorm. Then lightning explodes all around Josh in bright dancing *bolts* that spurt from the cloud. A few stray *bolts* reach the ceiling, and one reaches only a couple of yards away from us bystanders. A couple almost hit John, but he evades them as he swiftly retreats backward. I think that Josh redirects the *bolts* that get too close to John, though, because they are more angular than usual.

"Time!"

The *bolts* fade away while the cloud of *earth* dissipates with them, revealing Josh sitting still and relaxed on the floor with his legs crossed and his hands on the ground, palms up. Free from the chaos that swarmed him, Josh comes out of his statue position and stands up. John walks back to Josh to exchange a few words. They shake hands and then return to the line, talking along the way.

People in the line are chattering. I suppose they are slightly aghast at the little stunt that Josh pulled when his *bolts* came so close to us.

Walter steps forward from the line and faces us again. "Sophie and David."

My heart leaps with nerves and excitement. It is my turn to battle, and I am facing David. He seems considerably nice, but I have to ensure that I am nice in return. Though these people have experience in countering us, they still do not know what we are truly capable of. That is why everyone is so shocked by Josh's lightning storm.

David and I step forward from the line, and Walter reminds David to take it easy on me as we progress to the duel positions. Approaching Josh and John, I hear them replaying elements of their duel in lighthearted banter.

Josh smiles at me as they pass between us. "Go get him, Sophie," he whispers, just close enough so that I can hear him. I look back at him and see him continuing his conversation with John like they are buddies as they return to the line.

Nearing my position, I consider the battle that I am about to engage in. I do not know what David can do, but I do know what I can do, and my *ability* is considerably strong ... I think. I have to be mindful to be restrained, though, because I am sure that David plans to do the same with me.

No branches, I think. I should probably refrain from hand-to-hand combat as well. I do not know if I can even get that close to David anyway. It would depend on his *ability*. I realize that I am at a disadvantage. While it is always good to know your opponent in combat, I know absolutely nothing about David's *ability*. All I know is that it must be very well trained.

I reach the position that Josh was in, and David is all the way on the other side, where John was. The distance between the two contestants seems farther now than it did while I was watching in line with the other spectators. I am glad, though, because I need the distance in order to become acclimated to this training exercise.

I flex my *field* in my hands, unsure of who will strike first. At home, we were always taught not to be afraid to strike first but to always ensure that we were protected. I project my *field* around myself in a protective bubble and intend to grab David with my *field*.

I have barely budged a finger when something hits my *field*. It came from somewhere above and to my left. I look up, but I do not see anything. Something hits my *field* from the right, but I still do not see anything. I look at David, who has not moved, and I wonder if I am facing something other than David.

Then an onslaught of forceful hits showers down on my *field*, and something stings my left shoulder and then my right arm. Something that resembles a burn forms on my left shoulder, and I wonder how something could have reached me. My right arm is developing a mark too. Somehow David has gotten through my *field*. And the first two hits enabled subsequent attacks to penetrate my *field*, meaning that this onslaught could eat away at my entire shield.

I quickly flex my *field* in my hands, ensuring that it is still intact and functional as I release my bubble of protection and swiftly fling my right arm forward to throw a *field* around David. Just before it grabs him, something hits it and forms a gap. I wrap the *field* around him anyway. I can feel his body inside my *field*—every bend and angle—but there are gaps in my *field* that weaken my hold on him. I shoot another *field* around him with my left hand just as the initial layer disappears from my right hand's grasp. I grab him again with my right hand only for the other to lose its grip as well. I cannot get a hold on him. Yet all along, he does not move. I realize the unpredictability of this match given our two invisible forces.

I am not accomplishing anything, and if I am going to overpower David, I need to move faster than he is able to follow. Even the smallest, simplest attack—when done fast enough—can make all the difference.

I release David to swiftly erect a wall of defense ahead of me, just to my left. Leaving one hand to complete and sustain the wall, I withdraw the other to slap David with my *field* using the back of my hand. I feel my *field* make contact and knock him a couple of feet to the right. As soon as he lands, I swoop my hand under him and throw him several feet to the left so that he lands in alignment with my wall of protection.

This reminds me of my fight with the Killer yesterday. I bombarded her with overwhelmingly rapid collisions with shelves that took place too quickly for her to gather her thoughts. It is difficult to move my *field* so fast—especially over this distance—and to control it in two places at once. Still, I push myself, and I concentrate.

David attempts to rise from his stomach as invisible pricks penetrate my wall of defense. Immediately I throw up a new, unscathed wall to my right with one hand and scoop him several feet to the right with my other. Thankfully, I barely carry him in my *field* when I scoop him, so I do not feel the strain of his weight, as I did while facing the horrific assassin yesterday.

David lands in line with my new protective wall and attempts to get up. Before he can gather himself or attack me, I throw a *field* around him. My right hand releases the protective wall to throw another layer around David. I consider squeezing him, but his *ability* may be most effective when it does not have to project beyond his own skin. I resort to squeezing the inner layer with my left hand while keeping the outer layer steady with my right. I feel his arms, legs, and head as though they were part of a small object directly in my hand.

He becomes more and more constricted and rigid. His arms are tight to his sides, and his legs squeeze together. I expect to feel something eat away at my *field*, but I feel nothing. I may not have found a weakness in the Killer, but it seems that I have found one in David. I take advantage of the upper hand, squeezing more, until I feel his throat.

I jolt back to my senses, remembering the need to be careful. I am not fighting a Killer or any other enemy. I am fighting David, and I am squeezing him way too tightly. I immediately loosen my grip on him. When I see him gasp from the constraint, I release him completely in alarm. I was hurting him, and I did not even realize it. *I am done fighting. I am absolutely done.*

"Time!"

I look at Walter, who I wish had called time a few moments earlier. I cannot really see anyone's face from here, but there seems to be a level of excitement among the spectators. I turn back to David and jog to him. He is rubbing his arms and shifting his weight from one leg to the other, bending them to regain fluidity.

"I am so sorry," I say.

"Oh." He waves his hand dismissively as he massages his arm. "Don't worry about it. It was a good fight. I didn't expect that from you."

This surprises me, considering David has seen us in combat before. "Why not?"

"Well, I can penetrate just about anything: visible or invisible." He tilts his head at me to hint at my invisible *force field* as he starts to walk back to the line. I walk with him. "Not a lot of people can figure out how to challenge me. It's particularly complex to contend with something you can't see."

In the background, I hear Walter call the next two contenders forward for battle. I do not hear their names, though.

"It usually gives me an advantage," David says. As if it is an afterthought, he adds, "You know what I mean?"

I nod. Of course I know what he means. I have the very same advantage with my invisible *ability*, only I have not had many opportunities to use it strategically in that way. I cannot even say that I have ever had that perspective before, but he is right. Nonetheless, something tells me that I will have plenty of opportunities to take advantage of it here in the Resistance.

David is still rubbing his arms. I feel awful and wonder if I can feel the throbbing in his arms with my *field*. I discreetly let it seep out of my hand and spread it over his head down to his unharmed neck, searching for any injuries. I sense nothing abnormal and am so grateful that I withdrew from him before I caused any damage there. I reach his shoulders, sensing no softly protruding swellings or tender spots with a throbbing heartbeat, though I can imagine that there are slight bruises. I reach David's upper arms where he has been rubbing and can easily feel the abnormally intense heat radiating from them and his heartbeat pulsating in them.

We approach the next contenders, Jules and Margaret. Jules and I nod at one another in acknowledgment. She appears to already be in her Conqueror mindset. Her face and her steps are a little too tight. Margaret walks as though this will be a breeze for her—and maybe even fun. I even notice a smile on her face in passing. Regardless, Jules is facing someone who she is familiar with rather than a powerful stranger. I am glad that Walter has paired us with the few people here who we have met.

"Um ..."

I start, having momentarily forgotten about David.

"Just so you know, while I have the *ability* to *deteriorate* surfaces, I can also feel them."

I do not understand what he is trying to say, but the feel of his body heat and heartbeat reminds me of my *field* around him. "Oh." I retract my *field* immediately, embarrassed. "I am sorry. I just wanted to make sure that you are all right. I did not realize that I had squeezed so tightly."

David chuckles briefly before he pulls up short in pain. "Don't worry about it." He winces.

We return to the line, and I go back to my place in the corner. Jules and Margaret are still walking to their duel positions. I recall parts of my duel with David and wonder how Jules's duel will go. Like me—and Josh—Jules has no idea what her opponent is capable of. However, I am sure that Margaret knows what Jules can do. Still, Jules is a fast learner, just as Josh and I are. The advantages and disadvantages of Jules's duel swarm in my mind until the two contestants reach their stations. Jules is where I stood, and Margaret stands on the other side of the room.

After a quick moment, Jules jerks her arms into action, erecting three large pillars of *ice* across the center of the duel field, one after the other, between her and her opponent. She could have simply *encased* Margaret, but she is probably aware that Margaret is too well trained to allow that to happen. Besides, Jules needs a form of defense, and a minute threat such as this should result in a counterattack from Margaret that will show Jules what Margaret's *ability* is and demonstrate her fighting technique.

Jules awaits Margaret's reaction, but Margaret does not move. Suddenly, a red light shoots through an *ice* pillar and hits Jules in the chest, knocking her to the ground. I look back at Margaret, who has lunged forward in the blink of an eye with her hand held out and aimed at the *ice* pillar. I did not even see her move. Margaret quickly returns to her relaxed stance, with her legs apart and her arms hanging limp at her sides, as Jules gets back up with a hand held to her chest.

In a single fluid motion, Jules rises from a squat and throws a thin icicle through an *ice* pillar with her free hand. A mini *ice* storm is thrust out right behind it, through the pillar, just as the upper half of the pillar falls into the new gap, maintaining Jules's defense. In the same instant, Margaret's hands fly up to slice the initial icicle with a red line and split the line into a vertical plane of intricate red webbing that solidifies into a wall, melting the *ice* storm right behind it. Margaret's *ability* must deal with *laser beams* of some sort.

Still holding her hand to her chest, Jules has sliced down and through her central pillar with a sheet of *ice* as though wielding a curved blade. Parting her hand from her chest, she pushes the liberated half of her pillar at Margaret, simultaneously erecting an *ice* case around Margaret with the other hand.

Margaret creates another web of red *laser beams*, which do nothing to the pillar but reflect in various angles. A stray *beam* almost hits Jules, but she releases her hold on the airborne *ice* pillar to grab her chest again and leap out of the way just in time, dropping the *ice* pillar to the ground just before it hits Margaret. Jules has maintained the growing case of *ice* enveloping Margaret, though, and Margaret retracts her *lasers* from the dropped pillar, frantically looking around at the case as it comes to a point over her head.

For a moment, there is stillness, and the battle seems to be over. The *lasers* are gone, and no one has ever broken through Jules's thick *ice* cases before. However, there could always be an exception.

Jules walks cautiously toward Margaret, pausing at the gap between her two standing pillars of protection. Everything remains still, so she steps over the stump of her middle pillar and takes another vigilant step forward. Then she takes another. At the landing of the next step, a red glow emanates from within the *ice* casing and explodes into red *lasers* all throughout the room at random angles, as though Jules had just stepped on a trigger.

Jules hops around, avoiding the sudden *lasers*, until she

reaches a safe location. She has to stay bent at the waist in order to avoid a particular *laser beam* hovering over her. The *ice* case around Margaret is unchanged but now contains numerous red lines that appear distorted and blurred by the *ice*.

Jules glances around at the *beams* and creates a small block of *ice* in one hand. She sends the block to her right, gently intercepting the path of the nearby *beam*, and rotates the *ice* very slowly to carefully angle the *beam* away from her. She straightens herself up safely, and she emits streams of *ice* from her hands, which hang safely at her sides. The streams reach near Margaret and transfigure into tall sheets of *ice* that intercept more *beams*. Jules adjusts them slowly so that other *beams* that threaten her are angled away from her as well.

"Time!"

Jules freezes in the middle of adjusting her *ice* mirrors but then resumes adjusting them. I know that it is not out of disrespect for Walter, though. Jules's *ice* cases are extremely thick, so Margaret may not have heard Walter call an end to the match. She needs to be freed before we can be sure that she is aware of the battle's conclusion, and thus far, Jules is the only one who can melt her *ice* cases. Walter seems to understand, because he makes no effort to protest or question what Jules is doing.

Jules successfully manages to create a clear path between herself and Margaret and walks to her. Though I try not to, I feel slightly tense, because this can be severely dangerous. Margaret could burst out with an attack upon being freed, completely unaware that the duel is over, or the *beams* inside the case with Margaret could rearrange themselves into precarious angles with the disappearance of the *ice*.

Jules tentatively touches the tip of the case, and the *ice* begins to melt. Immediately, Jules forms an abnormally thick sheet of *ice* between them, at least half a foot thick, and steps back from the moving *beams*.

She stops abruptly, however, and looks behind her when she realizes what is happening. Melting the case not only alters the angles of the *beams* inside the *ice* but also confuses the angles of the *beams* behind her. She is trapped in a battlefield of dancing *laser beams* that obliterate the safe, clear path that she just created. And they will sear her.

I throw my *field* at her, though I know that it will not reach her in time.

Chapter 9

I UNINTENTIONALLY STOP MY *field*'s advance in surprise when two people rise from the ground at Jules's side with arms around each other's shoulders. One of them immediately touches Margaret's shoulder, and the *beams* fade away. Jules is safe. I retract my *field* as the two rescuers gather Jules and Margaret together and sink into the earth. I do not need to see them resurface in front of the line, where Walter usually stands, to know who the two rescuers are. There is only one person I know who can manipulate the earth, and only one person I know who can *deteriorate abilities*. I just did not know that an *ability* could be shared with other people.

Something that Walter said about Blue Light comes to mind. He said that it takes a person beyond their limitations—that if their *ability* is to *camouflage*, for instance, then perhaps Blue Light could help them *camouflage* others as well.

Margaret holds her arms to her chest, recovering from the cold, and looks around like she is still familiarizing herself with unfamiliar surroundings. John escorts her back to the line while Jules speaks with David, holding her chest with her hand again. She must be hurt.

Walter meets Margaret and John as they approach the line. He speaks with them very briefly and then proceeds to Jules and David. After a short conversation, David escorts Jules to the stairs to leave. I want to go with them, but I also do not want to disrupt the way things are done here and leave training early if I do not need to. We are expected to be here, and I trust that they will take good care of Jules until I see her after the session. So, I stay.

Walter faces the line and resumes the training session. More duels take place. I do not know if everyone gets a turn to compete. I am frequently distracted by thoughts about Jules and Blue Light Energy. For something to be as helpful and as powerful as Walter described Blue Light Energy to be, it only seems natural to find it intriguing. I wonder how often people resort to using Blue Light and how much Jules, Josh, and I were set at a disadvantage when facing our opponents, who already knew how to use it. Most of all, I wonder when we will begin to train with Blue Light Energy.

"That concludes our duel session for today," Walter says to the line. "You are dismissed until it is time for lunch."

Everyone maneuvers to the stairs, and I follow the line. Ahead, Walter is speaking with Josh, who then walks up the stairs with everyone else. As I pass Walter, he lightly touches my shoulder.

"Jules is in the medical wing. The injury is minor, but David took her down to tend to the burn."

I nod at him. I knew that she was hurt, so this does not surprise me.

"If you would like, I can escort you there."

I wonder why Josh is not coming with us, but then I remember where Jules was hit and think that it is probably best. "I would appreciate that."

Walter nods and turns to lead the way up the stairs behind everyone else who has just left the room. Entering the staircase, I notice that the torch Walter brought down here is missing from its sconce. Someone must have taken it upstairs already.

The echoes of feet shuffling against stone still reverberate in my ears throughout the staircase, like in a stone tunnel. The rough-hewn stone constantly reminds me of the forsaken mansion, and I wonder how many times I will have to walk through this staircase before that mansion no longer comes to mind. Once we reach the top of the staircase, I see the torch replaced in its original sconce.

We come out to the main lobby, returning to the furnished and polished appearance of the mansion. People ascend the tall staircases on either side of us, and a few traverse through the archway to the lounge area, perhaps to rest or to stop by the kitchen for something to eat. Again, I do not notice anyone go through the archway on the other side of the foyer. I suppose between the forbidden narrow staircase and Walter's office area—if that is what it is—no one has reason to go down that hallway.

I follow Walter through a doorway into a dark, narrow walkway under the staircase to our right. Walter touches something on the wall that brings to life dull lighting just above our heads in the ceiling. I follow Walter forward as the dull lights sequentially illuminate the walkway. The procession stops at a door a few yards ahead of us.

The walls are a rusty color that I cannot clearly see because of the dim lighting. The floor appears to be rough stone, like the spiral staircase. This is the second passageway I have come across that does not match the appearance of the rest of the mansion. I wonder how much work Walter did on this place and if it was Walter who did the work at all.

As we reach the short walkway's end, the door opens, and white light pours into the passageway. The room beyond the door is like the sun compared to the walkway. Through the slight opening, white-tiled floors and white walls peek out at us, along with David's head. He must have heard us.

He opens the door all the way when he sees us and steps aside to let me through. Walter stays behind in the walkway and speaks with David about something that I do not listen to.

The room looks small and bland but sterile. A tall metal cabinet stands in the far corner in front of me, and white cabinets surround the room, containing seemingly limitless concoctions and healing supplies. In the center of the room stands a white medical bed that Jules is sitting on, tended to by a woman dressed in a pair of jeans and a small black shirt, who I suppose is a sort of nurse or doctor for the Resistance.

Jules's top is off. It sits at the foot of the bed while she sits at the head of it, facing away from the door, and the woman applies bandages to her burn. I hope that David was by that door this entire time.

The female medic looks up at me and smiles. "Hello," she

says brightly.

"Hi," I reply.

"Hey, Soph," Jules says when she sees me come around the bed to face her.

"Hey. Are you all right?"

"Yes, I am fine. Margaret just got a lucky hit during the match. She would not have gotten that far had I known what *gift* she had."

I find myself stealing a glance at the door to ensure that David and Walter have their eyes safely away from Jules. She can handle herself, without a doubt, but I cannot help feeling protective of her. We are like sisters.

Jules notices the twitch in my attention and waves her hand dismissively. "Do not worry about them. David has been standing at that door, facing the wall, ever since we got here."

"Why is he still here?" I do not mean it unkindly, but I am sincerely curious as to why he has stayed here to stare at a wall.

Jules shrugs nonchalantly. "He wanted to make sure that I was all right." She does not say it, but knowing Jules, I am sure that she could not care less if David stayed to stare at a wall, or if he left. It is his decision to deal with—not hers.

"Well, that's it," the woman coos, stepping back from Jules. She reaches over and grabs Jules's top to hand it to her.

Putting on her shirt, Jules asks, "How did your match feel?"

I am taken aback by her unexpected question. "It was … very involved. I think I forgot that I was only in a training exercise."

She nods. "Yes, well, I practically had to. Otherwise, I would probably be charred to ash by now. Where is Margaret, anyway? She looked a little shaken up last I saw her."

"I have no idea. I saw a few people go upstairs and some go into the lounge area. She may be in one of those two places."

She nods. "Did anyone else's duel get as … involved as ours?"

I frown and shake my head bashfully. "I was not really paying a lot of attention after you left." I do not want to say that I was thinking about Blue Light in front of these people. It does not feel right telling them that I have been contemplating their essential *ability*.

Jules does not pry any further regarding my apparent distraction, and I am glad. Instead, she looks up at the medic. "Thank you," she says.

"Of course! Try not to get yourself killed, though, okay?" she teases.

"Oh, I will," Jules says with a fervent determination in her tone that I am sure carries more than what is explicitly stated.

I smirk at her and grab her arm teasingly. "Come on."

She slides off the bed and comes with me to the door. "It was nice to meet you," Jules says, waving over her shoulder at the woman.

We approach David and Walter.

"Are you okay?" David asks.

"Yes, I am fine," Jules replies. "Are the duels still going on?" she asks Walter.

"No, we just finished," he responds. "Everyone is just hanging around right now."

"So, we go back to our rooms?" I ask him.

"If you wish," he says. "Your permanent residence should be ready for you by the end of the day. Until then, I apologize for the inconvenience of your present accommodation."

"All right," Jules and I say.

Walter is so preoccupied with our comfort in the kindest way, but it really is unnecessary.

"Where is Josh?" Jules asks.

"I sent him up with everyone else," Walter says. "I informed him that you were here, but I suggested that he return to your temporary room while you were being tended to."

"Oh," she mouths, and then she turns to David. "Thank you—for bringing me up here."

His face spreads into a smile. "You're welcome, but be careful, especially with Margaret. She is not one to go easy on people."

"Yes, I have noticed," Jules says.

"Just … try not to get yourself killed, okay?"

Jules throws up her hands in mock disbelief. "How many people are going to tell me that?"

I laugh. "Come on. We should let Josh know that you are all right."

"Wait," Walter says. He takes out his keys and fumbles with them. "Here." He gives us a gold key. "Josh has one as well. I think that two should be sufficient, considering you will not be staying in that room for long—unless you want another one?"

"It is fine, Walter," I say. "Two is enough. Thank you."

"Do you remember which room you are in?"

I think back to the empty golden slot next to our door. I do not know how many doors there are in that corridor, but I do know which one is ours. "Yes, we will be fine."

Walter nods. "Lunch is in an hour, and then we usually break off into individual training. I want to speak with the three of you then."

Jules and I nod in agreement.

Walter steps aside and gestures for us to go ahead to our room. We walk past him, saying goodbye to him and David, and step into the walkway to proceed to our room.

"Hey, Jules! How are you feeling?"

I close the door behind me and meet Josh and Jules in the bedroom.

Jules waves her hand in nonchalance. "I am fine. I am fine. It was just a little burn. That is all."

Josh is reclining on the bed that Jules slept in last night, propped up against the pillows. Jules walks between the beds and sits on the other one. It reminds me of how they were sitting last night during our first opportunity to relax in a long time. I come in and sit on the end of the nearest bed, near Jules.

"Margaret got you pretty hard, huh?"

Jules looks insulted. "She did not. She took advantage of my ignorance." Josh laughs as Jules becomes defensive. "I did not know what *gift* she has, and instead of going easy on me, she attacked me with full force. I do not mind her eagerness in the fight, but the least she could have done was work me up to it."

"Jules, I think she did go easy on you," I say.

"Soph, you heard David. Margaret is not one to take it easy on people."

This time I am the one who laughs. "Yes, but I think that he was partially joking. Besides, you love a challenge, and she already knew how fast you are and how strong your *ability* is. We may not be as well trained as these people here are, but we definitely have substantial training."

Jules shrugs and looks away at Josh. With wide eyes and a sassy tone, she dramatically admits, "This is true."

"What are we going to do with her?" I ask Josh.

Josh just shakes his head and laughs. "What about you? How are you holding up after your session? You seemed to hit David pretty hard."

My eyes widen when I am hit with a pang of realization.

Josh's face becomes cloaked in concern. "What is it?"

"I saw David right after the session let out, and I did not even ask him if he was all right. It completely slipped my mind. I guess I was so lost in my thoughts after Jules left that I completely forgot about my duel with David."

"Oh."

"Well, I am sure that he is fine, Soph," Jules says. "He did not even bother to get examined while we were in the medical wing."

"Right, but we left before he did."

"Oh," she says.

"I am going back downstairs." I need check on him. I have been smacked around before, and I know that it does not feel good and can cause serious injuries. I get up to leave.

"Soph, wait," Josh says. "Are you sure that is such a good idea?"

"Why would it not be?"

"If he is getting treated for any injuries, you should give him his privacy. After that, he will probably go to his room. We have an hour to relax. Let him recover, and you can ask him at lunch."

Josh is probably right, as usual. I should wait.

I sigh submissively. "All right." I settle back down on the bed. "So, Jules and I were not the only ones who seemed to fight a little hard during our duels. What was that last stunt you pulled?"

"Yes," Jules agrees, "that is exactly what I would like to know."

The truth is, our matches were supposed to be simpler than everyone else's. Walter told our opponents to go easy on us, but all three of our matches seemed to get more intense than anticipated.

"What? John was burying me in *dirt*."

I obviously know this, but I throw him a dubious look

anyway, just to mess with him.

"Fine, you try being buried alive—literally—and then you two come back to me. He is persistent. He got *dirt* in my eyes—*dirt* in my ears. It was infuriating."

"What happened to the *dirt* that was in your eyes? You *bolted* it out?" I tease.

"Well, no, actually. I tried tearing up while walking back from the match, but not enough tears came for all of the particles to come out. When I returned to the line and saw Jules"—he nods in her direction—"I asked her to splash them out."

"Oh, Josh," I say condescendingly. "That is cheating."

He shrugs innocently.

"And you," I turn to Jules. "How could you let him resort to a 'resource' other than his *gift* like that? Not only did he use a different resource, but he used someone else's." I click my tongue three times in disappointment. "Shame, shame, shame," I say, wagging my finger at her in mock chastisement.

She looks at me blankly. "Wow. Yet you ask what to do with me?" she asks, pointing to herself.

I smile at her, and I turn to the both of them. "What other kinds of resources do you think these people have, anyway?"

Jules shrugs.

"Well," Josh says, "there are our *branches* and our advanced physical strength. Everyone has that. The people here apparently also have the Blue Light Energy that Walter spoke to us about last night. On top of that, they would have *abilities* that are signature to their origins. I do not know what divisions or other homelands these people are from, though. Conquest, obviously, had *signaling* as its signature *capability*. Diligence has some kind of control over body molecules, I believe ..."

"And Victory has a sort of mental *capability*," Jules adds. "It has something to do with reading minds, I think, or maybe they control something. I am really not sure."

Josh nods. "As for anything else, I really do not know."

"I wonder how many locations are represented here," I say.

Josh shrugs, uncertain. "There is really no way to tell at this point."

"Well, we will probably find everything out soon enough," Jules says. "Besides, Walter said he wants to speak with us after lunch."

"He did?" Josh asks.

I completely forgot that Josh was not there to hear Walter. "Yes, after lunch is individual training, and Walter wants to speak with us then," I inform him.

"Hmm."

"What?"

"I wonder if we are going to receive our first lesson on using Blue Light Energy."

I ponder this while enthusiastic anticipation warms my heart.

Apparently, I am not the only one who has been preoccupied with thoughts about Blue Light Energy.

Chapter 10

J OSH, JULES, AND I leave the room to go downstairs when we hear activity in the hallway. Doors open and close outside our room as stray conversations seep in through the door. We walk through the corridor and descend the staircase. Walking through the lounge area, we see people interacting on the furniture and by the windows while eating finger foods off mini plates. There is almost a regal presence to their leisure. We continue walking to the dining rooms.

"Jules!"

We whirl around to find Margaret getting up from the sofa, where she leaves John and David.

"Margaret!" Jules exclaims in surprise.

I did not even see them, and I am guessing that Jules and

Josh did not either. As Margaret approaches us, I realize why. She looks different. In fact, she wears an outfit that resembles what members of the Resistance wore last night, only this one appears to be more athletic. She wears a small black hoodie that is unzipped to show her fitted black top underneath and a pair of fitted black sweatpants. Everything is fitted so that nothing is loose or dragging.

David and John, who put their food down on the table in front of them and get up also, are dressed similarly. As they approach us, I examine David for any awkward patterns in his movement. I cannot use my *field*, because he will feel what I am doing, but I do not see him limping or holding his arm.

"I wanted to apologize to you for earlier today," Margaret tells Jules.

Jules looks at her and works her jaw like she is considering whether to accept her apology. Jules is only messing with Margaret, but I am concerned that it may be a little premature for Jules's humor to be thrust on these people. They do not know her very well yet, and I do not know if Margaret will understand—even though she carries herself in an audacious, confident manner that reminds me a lot of Jules. Nonetheless, despite the lack of familiarity, Jules will still be herself, because she has no intention of changing who she is for anyone—not even for a moment.

"All right," Jules concedes animatedly, as though she has just reached a verdict. "I will forgive you." She leans in as though to tell Margaret something confidential and softly adds, "But be careful where you stand. The next battle, I will not be so easy on you."

Jules is warning Margaret to watch her feet. During their duel, Margaret was too distracted by Jules's *ice* pillar to notice the case of *ice* building up around her.

To my surprise, recognition flashes across Margaret's face, showing that she understands Jules's reference. "I'm sure," Margaret counters in friendly banter.

Jules and Margaret appear to have a similar sense of humor, and something tells me that this will be a wonderful relationship.

"What is the occasion?" Josh asks, gesturing to Margaret's ensemble.

Margaret looks down at her clothes. "Oh. We're going on a stakeout tonight."

"A stakeout?" Jules asks.

"You go on stakeouts?" Josh asks.

Margaret looks insulted. "Well, just because I'm a female doesn't mean I can't handle myself."

"That is not what we mean," Josh explains. "Why do you go on stakeouts?"

As David and John reach Margaret's side, John crosses his arms. "A resistance that doesn't do stakeouts," he ponders sarcastically. "Nope, doesn't sound right to me."

David looks annoyed for us. "We go out to investigate the perimeter. We have top-notch security around the mansion, but we check up on everything just to make sure."

"You have to be that stealthily dressed for a perimeter check around your own land?" Josh asks.

"Well … then we're going near the compound."

"The compound," Jules repeats dubiously.

"As in the Fireburst Compound?" I ask.

"Yeah," Margaret answers.

"Why are you going there?" I ask.

Margaret, David, and John exchange looks, and I wonder why the matter is so secretive.

Margaret hesitates before answering. "You should probably ask Walter."

Walter said that he wanted to speak with us after lunch. Hopefully, it will pertain to this mysterious outing.

I consider asking David how he is feeling, but now does not feel like the right time. Besides, for him to be going on a stakeout, he must be relatively well. I would think that Walter would not have David engage in something so physical if he were injured.

Josh, Jules, and I agree to consult Watler, and we proceed through the doors to the dining room to get something to eat while Margret, John, and David return to their food by the couch.

Inside the busy dining room, food is laid out on small, revolving silver platters along the length of the long table. Some platters are layered, while others are simply individual. The platters feature finger foods that I am not familiar with but that look appetizing. Some platters also have mini pastries that appear to involve chocolate, icing, and dough baked into crusts. Large dishes sit among the platters and hold cheesy delicacies and some kind of meat. Everything appears to be somewhat elegant but casual when factoring in the banter and manner in which everyone grabs their food, like this morning.

There are a few vacant seats, but they are scattered. There are no available seats in a group of three. We decide to try the other dining room. Walking through the kitchen, we see a few people busy cleaning up pots and pans and other culinary equipment. Walter is busily working among them, putting things away. We pass on to the next dining room and find it practically empty, which is probably because a number of people are in the lounge area. The few people who could not fit in the other dining room probably came in here.

A woman sits at the near end of the table, talking to another woman and a man sitting across from her. This place seems to be built on groups of three. And these three individuals are dressed like Margaret, John, and David, wearing tactical black attire. Plates and silverware are situated along the table, but there is not a lot of food, which I presume is because barely anyone is here. The only platters and dishes in this dining room are situated by the three people who are already here.

Josh and Jules travel along either side of the table, but I stop by the group along the way to ask for a couple of dishes, since they already have their food distributed on their plates. They kindly nod in consent, and I bring a meat dish, some cooked grain, and a cheesy dish to Josh and Jules, seated at the middle of the table.

"Enjoy," I say, placing the dishes between them and sitting down next to Jules.

"What is this?" Jules asks as she sinks a serving utensil that was set on the table into the cheesy dish.

"Um ..." I rack my brain for an answer, but I am at a loss.

"It is a spinach and cheese casserole delicacy," Josh says. "My mother used to make it on certain occasions."

He sounds excited, so it must be an exceptionally delicious dish. I just do not remember it among her dishes that I have eaten. Jules does not seem to remember it either. Perhaps we never got a chance to taste it.

"What is the meat dish?" Jules asks, adding it to her plate.

"Mmm." Josh tries to speak through his mouthful of casserole. "Moose."

"Really?" I say, adding it to mine. "It looks different." We used to eat moose at home for dinner sometimes, but it was prepared differently. At home, it was made with a thick gravy, whereas this dish is dressed in a bright orange sauce and accompanied by vegetables and fresh seasonings.

"It is probably just the sauce," he says. He takes a bite out of it, and his eyes brighten. "It tastes remarkable. It actually tastes better than at home. It is different, but it is definitely moose."

Jules and I hastily take a bite. Josh is right. It is moose, and it is better.

"Wow," I utter.

"I would say," comments Jules.

Josh smiles around a mouthful of food and dives back into his plate.

"Excuse me," the woman who I asked for the food calls.

"Would you guys like a pastry?" She gestures to a layered platter near her.

"Yes."

"Please," I agree with Jules.

Josh is too busy eating to say anything.

The woman takes the platter and brings it to us. I cannot see her face very well, because her hood is pulled over her head so that it droops over her face. Similar to Margaret, she wears black pants that hug her frame. Her small hoodie is slightly unzipped, and the black shirt underneath hugs her torso. Wherever these people are going, it requires an allowance for fast movement and the epitome of stealth.

"Thank you," we say.

"No problem. I'm sorry to eavesdrop, but I heard you talking about the food."

"Yes, it is great," Jules says.

"Agreed. Josh would say so as well, but he is a little preoccupied, as you can see." I signal to Josh, who is stuffing his face in the politest way possible. Among the many things that Josh is good at, he is adept at eating and appreciating food, and we have not had good food like this in a while.

"I never really came across moose much at home—or the casserole," the woman says.

"Oh, really?" I say.

"Where are you from?" Jules sounds curious, but it does not completely conceal the eager tone in her voice from our conversation earlier about the different divisions represented here.

"Conquest," she says. I look at the woman, perplexed, and then I remember who I came across last night. The woman removes the hood from her head, and the light shines in the woman's—the girl's—big brown eyes.

"Delia!" I exclaim.

She chuckles. "Hi."

I had forgotten about her being here. There has been so much change going on for us—and I have just been so happy that we do not have to settle for a life on the run forever—that I had completely forgotten about Delia. I have not seen her since last night. I did not even see her downstairs in the training room—unless I missed her after Jules, or not everyone in the line competed in a duel after all.

"Oh," Jules says. "Hey, you are the girl from last night."

"Yes," I say. "I am sorry. I never properly introduced all of you. Jules, Josh, this is Delia. Delia, this is Jules and Josh."

"Yeah, I remember Jules from educational sessions back at home."

"We had class together?" Jules asks.

"Only for combat training," Delia responds. "You were one of the best students around. You kind of had a reputation." She turns to Josh. "I don't think I know you, though."

Josh takes a break from his moose and casserole. "I am from an older segment by a couple of years."

"Oh," Delia mouths.

It surprises me how freely she addresses these people who she does not know. The Delia that I knew would have been too shy to have a long conversation with a friend, let alone to address strangers. Once, I almost viewed myself as a big sister to her. I am only a few months older than her, but I always felt somewhat protective of her small and fragile stature for a Conqueror. I knew how shy she was and what made her nervous. I knew her weaknesses and her delights. I knew her efforts and her goals. Now I am completely unfamiliar with who she is. She is far more confident and ... free. Even her speech is freer and more fluid in an appealing, carefree way, similar to the speech of others in the Resistance. Everyone here seems to carry a certain confidence and have an authoritative aura to them—even this little blossom who has sprouted into such a bold radiance all of a sudden.

I realize that Delia is the woman who I noticed is furtively dressed, similar to others in the Resistance this afternoon.

"Delia?" Her attention returns to me. "Why are you dressed so surreptitiously?"

Delia shrugs a shoulder. "We're going out on an operation tonight." This is yet another vague answer, and I am not an advocate of her going on whatever assignment this is.

"What is the operation?" Jules asks.

Delia appears uncomfortable with the question, and I glare back at Jules, who tosses me a look as though to ask, *What?* It is evident that these people are restricted from saying too much about tonight to us. I do not want to pressure anyone about what is going on, and quite frankly, I do not believe that we should until we speak with Walter. I just wanted to confirm if Delia is participating in whatever is happening tonight, because I cannot imagine her doing something so potentially dangerous. I guess I still look at her as a younger sister—despite how independent she has become.

"It's just a run-of-the-mill perimeter check."

"Yes." Disappointment and exasperation resonate in Jules's voice. "We have heard that before."

I decide to change the subject. "Delia, how come I have not seen you all day? What about during the training exercise downstairs?"

"Oh, I don't go downstairs with the majority of people here. I can fight, but there's not a lot that I can do with my *ability* in that department. My *ability* isn't exactly meant for battle, if you follow," she says with a wink. "I train with my *ability* in another training room."

"Does anyone else train that way?" I ask.

"Oh, yeah. I'm not the only one with a mental *gift*." Her use of the word *"gift"* reminds me that she is from Conquest—that she is from home.

"What is your *gift*?" Josh asks.

I guess Josh did not hear that part of her story last night. Momentarily, Josh's furrowed eyebrows relax as he gradually stares deeper and deeper into space with a blank look on his face. He does not look at anyone. He does not return to his food. He is completely lost in the misty haze of his own mind.

"Josh?" Jules asks.

"He's fine," Delia says. "I just *clouded* him a little bit."

Josh suddenly blinks back into reality.

"See?"

A laugh furtively bubbles inside me. This new Delia is almost humorous to me. She not only seems like a different person; she seems like a person who would eat the old Delia alive. My mind quickly flashes back to my first encounter with her, several years ago. That frightened little girl would be a lion ready to pounce if I raised my voice at her like that now.

Once upon a time, Delia would never have used her *ability* on someone. She would only have used it *for* someone. Now she uses it on someone just to demonstrate what she can do. It is amusing, really. I wonder if she can enhance her *ability* to read people's minds or accomplish some other advancement through training or through Blue Light.

"Wow." Josh blinks a few times and then looks at Delia in astonishment. "That was you, I presume."

"You presume correctly," she responds brightly.

"That is incredible."

Delia looks pleased with herself as Josh speaks.

"I was just talking, and ... I do not know. There was nothing. I did not have a single thought in my mind. It was like nothing existed—even more so than when you are asleep. How long was I like that for?"

"About five seconds."

Josh appears confused. "That is it?"

Delia laughs. "Well, let me allow you guys to finish eating. You need your strength."

"Bye," we all call after her as she returns to the man and woman at the end of the table, and we return to our food.

"What is going on tonight?" Jules asks.

"I do not know," I answer, "but whatever it is, I am eager to hear what Walter has to say to us." As nice as Walter is, I question just how open he will be with us if he has gone through all these lengths to ensure that we could only find out about tonight through him.

Josh finishes his food and looks up to find us still eating. "You girls are slow."

"And you, boy, eat too fast for your own good," Jules says.

"Hey," I interject. "Can I eat in peace without you two competing for the Best Eater Award?"

Jules swiftly grabs a chocolaty morsel from the layered platter that Delia just brought over, swipes some chocolate off it with her finger, and I gasp when she smears it on my cheek.

"Mm-hmm. You see what happens when you tease me?" she says to the background music of Josh's laughter.

I glare at her through squinted eyes as I wipe my face with a napkin and then act casual. "Well, I suppose you are right, Jules. I should not tease you"—I casually place my hand on the edge of the table and let my *field* seep out from between my thumb and pointer finger to the pastry platter—"because teasing you apparently means you teasing me. And you know—" I use the subtle guidance of my pointer finger to throw a truffle at Jules's face, smearing chocolate on her nose.

"Uh!" she gasps.

I shrug innocently. "I just do not do well with being teased."

Josh is having a fit of laughter, and I chuckle with him as I put another forkful of moose and the casserole into my mouth.

"You—" Jules raises her hand.

I throw up a finger to stop her with my *field*. "Ah-ah-ah," I say, wagging my finger at her. "We are even," I sing. I release the *field* and return to my meal.

Jules gives in and returns to her plate as well. I look up at Josh and smile at him around a mouthful of food.

Soon Jules and I finish eating, and we take a couple of truffles as we get up to take our plates into the kitchen. Josh already ate a few truffles while we finished our food, but he takes a few more when we get up to leave. We walk along the table toward the kitchen.

"I'll see you later, Sophie," Delia says. To Josh and Jules, she says, "It was nice meeting you two."

Before they can respond, the woman that Delia is sitting with perks up. I recognize her stern, mature face. "Sophie? You three are the ones that we went after last night."

I try to draw a correlation between this woman's face and where I recognize it from, but I am not recalling it.

"And you are the one with the iron grip," Jules responds.

That is how I recognize the woman's face. She was the one holding Jules by the hedge last night. Jules does not sound bitter or upset. She just sounds neutral. My concern, however, is the woman. I am not sure if she is merely reflecting on our experience last night, like John did, or if she is actually hostile toward Jules. Judging by her reaction to Jules last night, I have reason to consider the latter.

The woman innocently raises her hands with a slight shrug. "Guilty."

"And I had your buddy," says a husky voice from the man next to her as his head nudges in Josh's direction. "How you doing, man?"

"I am good. How are you?"

"I'm fine. I'm fine. You three pack quite a punch."

"Yes, we have heard," Jules says in a cocky manner.

I look at her incredulously.

The woman silently chuckles at Jules's response. "Well, keep it up. I didn't know if you three would cause trouble, so I was pretty apprehensive about letting you go ... um ..."

"Jules," Jules finishes for her.

"Jules," the woman says in a satisfied conclusion. "My apologies."

Jules nods in acknowledgment.

"Same comes from me, man," the man next to the woman says. "Sorry …"

"Josh."

"Well, sorry, Josh. Hope there's no hard feelings."

Josh shakes his head. "There never were."

I think back to how nonchalantly Josh stood in front of the big man after he was released. He paid the man no attention. He simply stood there like it was no big deal.

The man nods a few times but looks like he is trying to get a read on Josh. "My name's Nathaniel. And this is Kate. I'm guessing you already know Delia."

"Yes, we have met," Jules says.

For some reason, I feel slightly uneasy with these two people, and I wonder how Delia became associated with them.

"Well, we should probably get these dishes into the kitchen," I say to Josh and Jules. I look back at Kate and Nathaniel. "It was nice meeting you two."

We say our salutations and take our dishes into the kitchen. As we put our dishes into the dishwasher, Walter approaches us from behind, wearing a black ensemble like several other people.

"Ah, there you three are. I was just looking for you. Everyone will be meeting in the private training facility. I want to train with you three separately from everyone else. We have a number of things to discuss. Some of us will be heading out tonight, so I will need to go over a few things with you."

He turns around to leave, but Jules stops him. "Wait, Walter."

He turns back to us.

"What is going on tonight?"

Walter hesitates before he responds. "That will be among the things that I will discuss with you in a few minutes. We will be heading up momentarily." With that, he walks off.

Jules turns back to me and Josh, and I just shrug. We still do not have any answers as to what is happening tonight—even Walter himself seems apprehensive to inform us of the plan—but at least he has committed to speaking with us about it in a few minutes.

As we begin to walk out of the kitchen, Margaret, David, and John enter.

"Hey," Margaret says. "Are you guys ready to go? We're leaving soon."

"Yes, we heard," I say. "We were just on our way out."

"Great," John cheers. "Now you little nippers can get more training so we don't have to keep going easy on you in communal training."

I realize for the first time just how much this place seems to be centered around training. So far, we have only experienced eating, training, resting, and more training.

"Ah, right," Josh comments sarcastically, "because a thunderstorm was so easy for you to match, right, John?"

John looks pointedly at Josh for a moment. "Like I said," he says. "Going easy."

"Oh, joy," Margaret complains. "Here we go again."

"I don't know, Mags," John responds. "I almost find it entertaining."

"'Mags'?" I ask. I like it. It sounds nice, and she looks like a "Mags" to me.

Margaret rolls her eyes, though, as if to say, *Don't entertain him.* She grabs me by the hands, tugging me forward. "Come on," she coaxes. "Let's go before John's ego suffocates us all."

Chapter 11

WE TRUDGE THROUGH THE first dining room, which is now empty, to get to the lounge area. More people have gathered in the room. Whereas before there could not have been more than eight people scattered in here, there are now over twenty. The majority are in regular clothes, but some are dressed in tactical attire. Pillars of black spot the crowd of people. Shortly after we arrive, the crowd begins to move. As we proceed out of the lounge area, I see Delia and her two friends coming from the kitchen.

I consider asking John, David, and Margaret about this private training facility, but I figure that we will reach it soon enough. Instead, I consider a better question that I have been waiting for the proper moment to ask. Walking through the lobby and up the nearest staircase, I move up next to David.

"Hi," I say.

"Hey."

"How are you feeling?"

He gives me a confused look, not understanding what I am referring to. I move to imitate how he was holding his arm earlier but think better of it as I am not trying to mock him. I resort to pointing.

His eyes follow my finger to his arm. "Oh, I'm fine. Don't worry about it."

I was sure that he would be all right, but I wanted to ask anyway. If nothing else, it was the right thing to do, and I am glad to know that I did not inflict any substantial harm.

"How's your arm and shoulder?" he asks.

At first, I do not know what he is talking about, but then I remember the penetration through my *field* and the marks on my arm and shoulder. "Oh. I completely forgot about them." I look down at my left shoulder, expecting to see a wound, but I see nothing. I check my right arm and find nothing there either. There is no trace of a mark anywhere, and I feel no pain at all. "There is ... nothing there."

"I know." He smiles. "I didn't strike you too badly, and I took it out when the match was over."

"You … took it out."

"Yeah, the mark only exists as long as my *ability* is in contact with a surface. I took it out while we were walking back."

"How did I not feel that?"

"You were probably too preoccupied checking to see if I was all right."

Of course. I was concentrating on exerting my *field* over David, searching for any bumps or bruises on our way back to the line, and he knew it. He probably removed his *ability* then, knowing that I would not even realize it. It was a neat trick.

"Very clever," I acknowledge.

"I thought you might think so."

We reach the top of the staircase and progress through the right archway, traveling down the hallway opposite where Jules, Josh, and I have been staying. This side of the corridor is a mirror image of the other side. It contains the same brown doors with golden-brown paper slots, the same white walls with curving patterns, and the same red-carpeted floor with golden patterns.

As I walk through the corridor, the mysterious subject of the operation tonight torments me, but I refuse to ask David or anyone else about it. Walter will speak to us about it soon, and no one else would be able to give me a clear answer, anyway.

The crowd pauses when it reaches the end of the corridor, probably because Walter has to unlock the door. Delia and her friends have kept a few yards' distance from the rest of the crowd. They never did catch up with us from when we left the lounge area. They have just followed behind the crowd at their own pace. When they have just about caught up with us, the crowd starts to move again.

Stepping through the brown door at the end of the hallway, we enter a dark space. To our left, a tall shadow reaches all the way to the ceiling. The lights suddenly flash on, and as the crowd disperses, I can see the large space better. The square room is about three-quarters the size of the duel training area downstairs. The floor is made of wood, and a mirror stretches across the entire right wall. The other three walls are tan and appear bland in comparison to the golden patterns and various colors throughout the rest of the mansion. The tall structure to our left is a spiral staircase centered around a gray pole leading up to higher levels, which I cannot see too well from here. I can only glimpse a wall of mirrors in the room above us.

"Okay."

My attention jerks to the source of the voice: Walter. He is standing in the near corner to our right, by what looks to be a light switch, rubbing his hands together as though eager to begin.

"Choose your rooms," he says. "My team, we leave after two hours of training. This is both training and warm-up for you. We will meet in the foyer. Everyone else trains for the regular amount of time. Jules, Josh, and Sophie, stay down here with me. The rest of you will have to disperse among the floors above. Dismissed."

At that, everyone heads for the staircase and swarms up the stairs to the levels above us. I wonder how many levels there are. Judging by our location at the end of the hallway, I would guess that we are in one of the towers of the mansion. There could be a substantial number of floors above us.

"See ya," David says to me.

Margaret and John say goodbye to us as well, though John's salutation runs along the lines of "Get some training, will ya?" Delia and her friends pass, also addressing us as they skedaddle to the staircase. Pretty soon, it is just the three of us and Walter left in this room.

"This training facility is designed to help develop resources outside of just your *abilities*," Walter explains as he walks toward us. "*Capabilities* that are signature to your division, strength, hand-to-hand combat, and so on—they are all trained and developed right here." He parts his arms above like a budding flower to encompass the totality of the room. "We will start with hand-to-hand combat, but first I need to speak with you in regard to a pressing matter. I am sure that you have heard a few snippets about tonight."

"Yes," we all say in unison.

Walter nods at the confirmation. "And no doubt you have noticed that some of us are dressed similarly to how we were dressed last night. No one has told you what we are doing tonight, in accordance with my ever-standing instructions not to confide in anyone regarding our operations until I make it clear that they are to be trusted. This applies to everyone and is for everyone—to keep everyone safe and ensure the protection of our clandestine efforts." He takes a breath in and then lets it out. "We go out for various reasons in pursuit of several objectives. Chaos is erupting. Divisions are being overthrown, destroyed, obliterated. Forests and sacred treasures are being devoured in fires. Your home is only one example of the many cases of destruction taking place."

Before Conquest was attacked by the Firebursts, rumors of a resistance were not the only things we heard. We heard of destruction brewing, but it was always at far distances away from us. We were unaffected by the uproar that was happening. What we did not know was that the disruption would arrive on our doorstep overnight. One day, it was thousands of miles away. The next thing we knew, we were all on fire. We thought that we had time to resist or that the problem would not spread so far to reach us. We were sadly mistaken. In the blink of an eye, it was all over and going up in flames.

"Where there is destruction, there may be stragglers," Walter continues.

I remember Walter telling us that some of the Resistance members are from destroyed divisions. Perhaps that explains the peculiarity of Delia's friends.

"We go out for stragglers—similar to what we did for you. Some nights we go out to stock up on supplies. Tonight, in particular, we are going on a stakeout at the Fireburst Compound."

My heart leaps in my chest. They really are going to the compound? Jules looks at Walter steadily with a neutral expression, hiding her internal thoughts, but I can see the masked worry on Josh's face when we exchange glances for an instant.

Walter seems to notice our concern but continues, probably hoping to effectively talk us out of our worries. "We plan on storming the compound soon, and we need to know the layout of the structure. We need to find out as much as we can, so this operation needs to go flawlessly."

They are mad. They really are insane. I understand that this is a resistance and that they are all very well trained. I also understand that as a resistance, they have to do something other than train and twiddle their thumbs all day long, but there has to be something that they can do outside of storming the Fireburst Compound. That is beyond dangerous. It is fatal. Plus, there are numerous threats and dangers around the compound—ones that we have had to face during our escape.

"Walter, you cannot storm the compound," I say. "There is no way that you can go in there and come back out in one piece."

"Well, you three certainly did."

"Yes, but that was different. You know how that happened. That was under the covering of an Oracle, sent out by this divine Blue Light that you have told us about. And we had a Prophecy—we had an Envisionment—to cover us. We had assurance."

Walter appears to be intrigued by the fact that we had encountered a Prophecy.

"Right," Josh adds, "and there is nothing covering you all or guaranteeing your safety—unless there is something that we do not know about."

"No, there is no Oracle involved," Walter says.

"Then it is a death sentence," Jules says conclusively.

I begin to wonder if we are overstepping our boundaries as guests that have been kindly invited to stay here, but I do not care. These "kind" people will be covertly marching to their deaths if they try to storm the compound.

"Well, I thank you for your concern, but this has been decided long before you three arrived. It was established long before we knew anything about your case—long before the Oracle and long before a Prophecy or an Envisionment of any kind. We have decided to storm the compound—even without that 'covering.' Such guarantees of safety are not always available when facing dangers, but it does not mean that you should not stand against them."

"But, Walter, you do not understand. It is not just that you cannot storm the compound. You cannot go out tonight either," Jules says intensely. Walter goes silent, and Jules slightly softens her tone. "There are new threats out there."

I am a little surprised by her urgency. I do not think that Jules wants these people to die or dislikes them, but I was under the impression that she was still somewhat doubtful or indifferent toward the Resistance. It seems that she feels a stronger bond to them than I realized, though—that she is open to them and has welcomed it as a potential residence, maybe not quite as home but as something close to it. And this makes her adamantly concerned about its members.

Walter furrows his eyebrows. "What new threats?"

"Walter," Josh intercedes so that Jules does not have to retell the story of her encounter yesterday. "While Jules was escaping from the compound, she ran into a group of Killers. They chased her down for a while and would have gotten her if we had not *signaled* her out in time. Sophie ran into a Killer as well."

Walter's head jolts in surprise. "Killers? And what is *signaling*?"

"We can summon another person to our location," I explain.

"Ah, a skill that is distinct to your division, I presume."

"Yes."

He nods pensively and then returns to the concern of the imperative matter. "Killers?" he asks again, confounded.

"Yes," Josh and I say.

Jules simply nods.

I hope that this discussion is not too much for her. However, if it is, I am sure that she will surmount it.

"Why are they at the compound?"

"We do not know," I say. "We only know that they were after us, but we have no idea why or who sent them."

"They cannot be under the order of the Firebursts, though," Josh adds. "They would not send henchmen out to kill us. They would want to bring us back for further interrogation, and the only thing that Killers do is kill."

"This is true," Walter says pensively, cupping his chin in his hand with partially crossed arms. As he ponders the situation, I hope that he will terminate the stakeout. My heart sinks, though, when he says, "We will need to prepare."

That does not sound like he plans to call it off.

"What do you mean, prepare?" I ask accusatorially.

"For tonight," he answers calmly, and he walks past us to the staircase.

"Walter," Josh interrupts. "It is not safe."

"No," he says, facing us in front of the staircase. "It is not, but this is what we have trained for. I will return shortly. I am going to inform the team of potential complications that we will face tonight and to make sure that they prepare accordingly."

He disappears up the stairs, leaving the three of us in distress. A few silent seconds pass before any of us says anything.

"They are still going," I concede aloud in hopeless disbelief.

Josh nods slowly, burdened with the same incredulity. I begin to feel guilty, knowing that the Killers are probably there because of us. If it were not for us, they would probably not even be there, and Walter would not be walking the Resistance right into their murderous hands and wretched smirks.

I smother the guilt, because it is not going to help the situation. I am a Conqueror, and if something has no purpose, then there is no point in dwelling on it.

"What do we do?" I ask.

"We?" Jules repeats. "Nothing. We do absolutely nothing."

"But, Jules, we—"

"You heard him, Soph!" she explodes, exasperated. She cautiously glances up at the next floor to ensure that she is not audible to anyone else. "They have had the invasion planned long before we ever arrived. They have had lots of training. They are equipped. They will be fine!"

"You do not actually believe that, do you?" Josh asks softly, though we all already know the answer.

Jules looks at him for a moment and cools down before responding. "No," she concedes softly. She sighs hopelessly. "But what can we do? They are going ... and that is it."

Silence envelops us, though the only option is clear and evident.

"We have to go with them," I acknowledge.

Josh looks up at me and nods solemnly.

"You mean go back." Jules practically spits the statement out in disgust.

"Who would we be if we did not?" Josh asks, and he is right. We are Conquerors. We do not let people go into the fire alone. We are there for each other, and we stand together—strong—as a team and as a unit. Besides, it is the least that we can do for these people, who have welcomed us into their lives with such kind hospitality.

Jules's expression is clouded by a combination of fear and anger.

I rush over to her and touch her shoulder. "Hey. We will be all right. This time, you will have us with you. You will not be alone. We will have each other, and we will look out for each other—just like always."

Josh comes up beside me. "We do not even know if the Killers are still there, Jules. And if they are, we are still family." He gently grabs her arm. "And you know how Conquerors value family."

Jules nods. "More than anything ... in everything."

I smile at the familiar motto from home.

"Exactly," he says.

The three of us hug each other—tightly. We stay in a hug for a while before we let go, grateful that we have one another.

Something comes to my mind, though. "How will we get Walter to let us go?" I could be wrong, but I seriously doubt that he will let us go on this evening's operation when we only arrived last night and do not have the training—or Blue Light Energy—that everyone else here has.

"We will just have to convince him," Jules says with a look of determination in her eyes. When Jules is committed to something, it is not likely that she will fail at it.

"Agreed," Josh says. "We may not have Blue Light, but we do have a lot of training. I think that we can handle ourselves pretty well."

I think back to our encounters over the last couple of days and our training sessions at home. Each of us were known for being among the top fighters in our segment. And Josh was considered among the most clever and astute students in Conquest. We are exceptional and can certainly handle any circumstances we face.

I smile at my Conquest family. We will convince Walter to let us go tonight, and we will conquer every obstacle that comes in our way, just as we have done all along. This will be no different.

Chapter 12

WALTER DESCENDS THE STAIRCASE. "I am sorry to keep you waiting, but that was an urgent notice that I needed to communicate to the team. I thank you very much for that crucial information," he says as he walks to us. "It is always good to have a warning. As for your training—"

"We are coming with you tonight," Jules informs him like there is no other option, which there is not.

Walter looks at us blankly. He is speechless for a moment. "Wh—uh—" He clears his throat. "That is out of the question."

He sounds oddly stern. It takes me aback a little. I am tempted to tell him that we are going regardless, but I doubt that will get us far.

"We are well trained," Josh reasons. "We can handle ourselves. Jules has faced a legion of Killers. Sophie has faced a Killer in direct combat."

I choose not to be tormented by recollecting the event.

"We know how to fight. You saw us in our duels this morning, and we were holding back, expecting that our opponents would be doing the same."

Walter ponders Josh's words. What he does not know is that whether he agrees to this or not, we are going. Even if we have to sneak onto this covert mission, we are going. I consider mentioning to Walter that joining this quest is the least that we can do for all his hospitality, but I know that he will accept nothing in return—least of all something so dangerous.

"You say that this is what you have all trained for," Josh continues. "Well, this is what we trained for back at home. Besides, we have been inside the Fireburst Compound. We know of at least two entryways, and we know several tunnels and byways. Not to mention the fact that we know where we spotted Killers, and we know some of the area around the compound."

Josh's logic is flawless. Surely, the Resistance already knows certain things about the Fireburst Compound, like some of its land, if they have been there on stakeouts before, but we still carry an advantage. We have been on the inside. We know it on levels that most of these people—if not all of them—are completely unfamiliar with.

Moments tick by with Walter's chin cupped in his hand again. He opens his mouth to say something, but it hangs limply for a second before he says, "Let's see how you train."

He walks into the empty space of the room. "For example ..." He turns back to us and raises his arms at his sides to erect a four-foot pedestal on both sides of the room, which each support a statue head. "Can you grab these with your *branches*?"

I do not know how he managed to make these two pedestals appear when his *ability* deals with blending with the winds, but I do know that grabbing these heads is no challenge at all.

"Sophie," he calls. He gestures for me to stand in front of him. "If you would, please."

I give Josh and Jules a knowing glance and begin to walk to Walter. This is extremely simple, but I will proceed with Walter's examination to make him comfortable with our proficiency. It seems unlike Walter to give us a task so basic, though. Perhaps he will increase the difficulty of this test as we go along.

I stop in front of him and look confidently into his eyes. Then, instantaneously, I whip my hand out to my right and grab the head with a *branch*. It is a little dramatic, but I figure that it is a good idea to add some flair to the simple task and let Walter know that this is nothing for us. I whip out my left hand's *branch* to the other head, but as soon as my *branch* loops around the head, the pedestal and its statue are gone, only to reappear half a foot farther along the wall. I glance at Walter, who is smiling knowingly at me.

My attention returns to the head. I flex my *branch* like a muscle at the head again, but my *branch* wraps around itself yet again when the head moves even farther along the wall. It is moving a greater distance away from me, which makes sudden and precise movement of my *branch* a little more complicated. I have an urge to use the *branch* of my right hand to help, but it is already holding a statue head that I do not want to relinquish and risk having a harder time capturing it again. My left hand is on its own, and whatever happens, I have to get this head. Otherwise, Walter will not want us to go on the expedition tonight.

I form a large loop around the head with my *branch* and rapidly snap the loop to tighten it around the head, but the head gets away again, reappearing just outside the tightened loop. No matter what I do, if my *branch* comes near it, it disappears. I am tempted to use my *field*, but I know that I am not supposed to use anything other than my *branches*. I need to trap it, somehow, using my *branches*. There is a solution somewhere. I just need to find it.

Then I have an idea.

I extend an excessive amount of my *branch* from my wrist and make a loop around the head with the middle of it, leaving a substantial length in the loop's tail farther along the wall. As I tighten the *branch*, the head disappears, but I have already begun to contour the tail of the loop in anticipation of the moving pedestal. The head reappears a couple of feet farther along the wall, in the middle of my *branch*'s second loop, and I grab it before it can disappear again.

Looking up at Walter while holding my prizes, I realize that I have been squatting in order to reach around him for the troublesome statue head. My left arm is practically touching him. Walter smiles at me like this is a game that amuses him.

"You can release them now," he says.

Hesitant to release what I worked so hard to grab hold of, I carefully let the heads go and retract my *branches*, straightening myself. I turn around and walk back to the others.

"Jules," Walter calls from behind me.

I pass her on my way back, and it feels like the other training session all over again. She raises her eyebrows at me as if to say either *Wow* or *Here we go again.* I am not sure which. I reach Josh and turn back around to watch Jules.

"That looked harder than it seemed," he says.

"It was."

The left pedestal holding the statue head returns to its original location, and it is Jules's turn. She lunges for the left one first, entrapping it between both of her *branches*. Her right hand's *branch* is the one that catches the head, so she whips around, facing us, to grab the other head with her left *branch*. Just that quickly, she is done, but only because I showed her which statue would be more challenging to seize. She comes back, and Walter calls Josh.

"Cheat," I tease Jules.

"I had an advantage," she says in defense.

I smirk.

Josh tackles the right pedestal first, which now turns out to be the moving pedestal. He grabs it easily enough, though. As the head disappears, Josh prepares a loop in the air and brings it down over the head just as it reappears, before it can disappear again. He is a lot faster than Jules and I are. Before I know it, he grabs the other head, which stands still—or he is too fast for it to move—and he is done.

"That was fast," comments Jules.

"As were you," I respond.

"Yes, but he had a surprise."

That is true.

Josh returns to join us.

"All right," Walter says as he approaches us with his hands clasped in front of him. "Very good." And he clearly means it. "Now, I want to see you in hand-to-hand combat. You will be training with me."

That sounds like a fair challenge. Hopefully, there will not be any unexpected complications this time.

"Jules, you and I will match first."

Jules steps forward, and they both walk to the center of the room.

Jules throws the first punch. She aims for his chest, but Walter blocks it and pushes it away with ease. She follows with another punch for his side, but he deflects that as well. She tries to knee him in the groin, but he blocks it. Jules advances with every strike, while Walter recedes with every block. Every block and grunt reverberates throughout the room. Each attack that Jules throws is a powerful one and met with an equally powerful block.

Walter retaliates with a few punches of his own, but he is clearly taking it easy on her. He is only trying to see how she handles them. Every attack she blocks cleanly. She performs a series of front and side kicks and executes a 360 kick, but he blocks or dodges every one of them. Jules does not quit, though. More advanced kicks and punches are exchanged between the two of them from various directions until Jules throws enough rapid attacks at him to land a powerful right hook to his face. She stops abruptly, and Walter looks back at her with his hand on his jaw.

"Very good," he says approvingly, and he gestures for her to return. Then he calls for Josh, the most trained of the three of us.

"How did I do?" she asks beside me.

"Not bad," I say, watching Josh advance toward Walter. I part my attention to give Jules a proud sideways glance. "I just hope that his jaw is okay."

Jules chokes back laughter at me, and I realize that she did not mean her question genuinely.

I chortle. "Oh. Sorry."

"He should be fine," she says confidently. "It was only a right hook. It was not even that hard. I was starting to get a little winded."

"I am sure."

Our attention returns to the match ahead of us, which has

already begun. Josh is pacing himself. He is not throwing rapid attacks yet. He is studying his opponent, examining Walter to see how he fights and what can be taken advantage of. A right hook is thrown here. A front kick is thrown there. A tornado kick swings at Walter after a while.

After a few blocked hits, Josh increases the pace and advances on Walter. The reverberating sound of his blocked attacks grows louder as he hits with greater force and speed. Walter has to block faster, moving quickly from left to right and below. Josh moves faster until he reaches Jules's pace, but his breathing is impeccable. I can barely even hear his grunts.

Walter retaliates with a few kicks and punches as well, but he does not go quite as easy on Josh as he did on Jules. He moves a little faster and inserts his attacks more frequently. Josh blocks them almost effortlessly. He does a 540 kick and misses when Walter dodges. He executes another advanced kick that lands in Walter's side and then swiftly comes back around with a kick that catches Walter in the chest. At that, Josh pulls up short.

Walter nods at Josh, clutching his chest and his side and appearing slightly winded after two consecutive matches. "Very good."

Josh turns around to come back as Walter straightens and calls me forward. I walk toward him and get a curt nod from

Josh as we pass.

I brace myself as I near Walter, reviewing certain weaknesses and advantages. He is already winded and becomes vulnerable when facing a plethora of attacks. I need to increase my speed exponentially at one point and to breathe properly in order to prevent myself from becoming winded.

I stop only a couple of feet in front of Walter with my legs apart. By instinct, I feel my *field* in my hands, because it is such a vital part of me—particularly in combat—but I let all that energy retract back up my arms and disperse throughout my body to my various muscles. This round of combat is meant solely for my fists and my kicks. I take a deep breath in and then let it—and all distractions and tension—out slowly to decrease my heart rate and relax.

Then my fists fly up, ready to fight, and a right hook flies to his torso. He blocks it, naturally. I do not use all my force just yet, because he will block me anyway. I am only testing my opponent. I throw in a low kick that he blocks and then aim a jump front kick at his head that he dodges, looking a little surprised. I gather that he gets alarmed by attacks near his head. My best bet is to aim high.

I pick up the pace. I throw a few quick punches, snap into a roundhouse kick, and then execute a skip side kick. I let him fall back in my advance and aim high with a tornado kick, landing it across his face.

I stop immediately, realizing that I have just kicked Walter very hard. That is at least the second hit to his face, but he recovers and gestures for me to continue.

I come a little closer hesitantly with my fists up and ready to continue. I consider what I want to do at this point. My breathing is a little fast, but I am not winded yet. I can afford to throw more intense attacks, but before I can, Walter throws a punch for my side, which I block. Another one comes for my other side. I dodge it and smoothly swivel into a 540 kick, kicking him somewhere that I do not see. I land and turn back around with my fists up, only to find Walter leaning to the side, holding his jaw again.

I freeze, staring at him, and then drop my fists. No matter what, I am done. If he is upset with my decision and will not let us come on the operation tonight, we will just sneak in among them.

I am grateful, however, when he comes back up and says, "Well done." In other words, *dismissed*.

A sigh of relief escapes from me, taking a heavy burden with it. Although sneaking among his team tonight would have been for their own benefit, I really did not want to have to betray Walter's trust that way. I turn, about to return to the others, but Walter tells me to wait and asks Josh and Jules to join us.

"You three have some very good training. Of course, I cannot see the totality of it in one day. Discovering the extent of such training requires time. It is a gradual process."

Otherwise, you could get hurt by overestimating your training is what he does not say.

"Nevertheless," Walter continues, "the skill that I have seen from you within the last twenty-four hours is impeccable. However, if we are potentially facing a considerable number of Killers, I doubt that your training will be sufficient." He puts up a hand to calm one of us, and I follow his gaze to Jules, who was just about to protest. "You would need greater tools," he finishes.

I examine Josh's and Jules's faces in my peripheral vision, wondering if they know what Walter is talking about. Something changes in Josh's face.

"We would need Blue Light," Josh acknowledges.

"Yes," Walter confirms.

"You are going to give it to us tonight?" I ask with eager anticipation in my heart.

Walter looks at me but pauses as though considering my

question or his answer. "No. I will teach you how to receive it yourself."

I recall Walter saying that one has to "request" Blue Light in order to obtain it. Excitement rises within me. Exactly what Blue Light is, I do not know, but one thing that I am learning about Walter is that I can trust him. Besides, Blue Light seems to be a remarkable force of energy to have.

"This is a lot sooner than I thought I would teach you," he says, "but circumstances seem to call for it right now. While you train with Blue Light, you will be able to do things that you could never do before. However, be sure that you never abuse it. Use it when you need it, but do not become greedy with it. The moment you veer to nefarious desires and ambitions, you will lose it—possibly forever. As I have said before, Blue Light only gravitates to pure hearts, so always keep that in mind."

We nod, heeding his instruction.

"All right," he says. "Close your eyes."

We do so, and I calm my heart as it pounds harder and faster in my chest.

"Feel your resources: your *abilities*, your *branches*, your division's signature *capability*, your strength, and your skills. Feel everything inside of you."

I obediently flex my *field* in my hands and my *branches* in my wrists, like muscles wriggling in my arms. I feel the power in my hands, in my arms, and in my legs. I feel the *ability* to *signal* Josh or Jules. I briefly allow myself to feel their heartbeats, their focus, and their anticipation. Josh's head is clear and purposeful, as usual, while Jules has thoughts that strongly recollect the icy flurries of her *ability* and glimpses of training exercises back home.

"Now imagine being able to do more than you could ever accomplish with them—being able to punch harder, to kick harder, to use your *ability* faster and project it better. To extend your *ability* to others so that they can use it, to extend multiple *branches* from a single hand, to use your division's *capability* in ways you never would have imagined. Expand your mind. Expand your skill. Expand yourself beyond every limitation and boundary that you could ever face."

It is an odd concept, but I imagine holding things in my *field* even after my hands have released them. I think of *signaling* people I do not know from great distances to my side. I envision myself running and not becoming fatigued. I visualize myself extending multiple *branches* from one hand, like Walter suggested. A trail of inconceivable visions and imaginings flows through my mind.

"Now accept it. Receive it. Welcome it and say, 'I invite you in.'"

"I invite you in," we say simultaneously.

"All right," Walter says.

A moment passes, and I wait with my eyes closed and with heart-throbbing expectation. I wait for Blue Light to hit me and make an astounding transformation. I expect to feel an astonishing power awaken in me that can demolish a building or support twenty people on my back. I do not feel anything, though, and Walter is silent.

"Open?" Jules asks.

"Yes," he says.

I open my eyes, but I am confused. I feel no different. I feel like the same person who was standing here a minute ago—the same person who faced David in the duel, who was scared and frightened yesterday, who struggled against a Killer, who was trapped in the Fireburst Compound, and who was raised in the now-demolished Conquest Division. I am not alone in my confusion. Josh and Jules appear perplexed as well.

"Walter," Josh says hesitantly. He turns his hands and his arms over, observing them. "Are we supposed to feel ... different ... somehow?"

"Not particularly, no. The change is on the inside. Though,

once you use it, it is clear for all to see in your *abilities*. You have to believe in it, though."

Josh looks at him questioningly.

"Try it," Walter urges.

Tentatively, Josh walks past Walter. "You have to believe in it," he mutters to himself, examining his hands again.

He stops between us and the back wall. After a moment of contemplation, he flings his arm up and then strikes it down to the floor. At the same time, a loud crackling noise thunders into existence, but it does not sound like it is in this room. I wonder if it comes from someone training upstairs.

"What was that?" Jules calls.

Josh turns around slowly, staring at his palms. "It was me," he says incredulously.

"What do you mean it was you?" she asks.

"I wanted to create something big—something bigger than I have ever done before—without extending it through my hand. I wanted to strike it down like lightning—almost like controlling the weather—and I just ..." He looks back at the opaque wall, and Walter is clearly pleased. "I made lightning."

I am speechless, and it seems like Jules is too. It is not impossible for me to have nothing to say, but for Jules to be speechless speaks volumes.

"Why don't you try, Jules?" Walter suggests.

Jules raises her eyebrows but turns around to slowly walk a short distance toward the room's entrance. She stops and suddenly whips her right hand out, expelling several *branches* from her wrist, which writhe in random directions. She does the same with the other hand, and it looks amazing. She flexes the *branches* around, testing them out and stretching them in different directions, until she swiftly retracts them into her wrists, snapping her fists closed and across her chest. She slowly pivots around to face us, bewilderment illuminating her face.

"Sophie?" Walter says.

Jules returns to us as I step forward. I know what I want to do, and I do not want to be near anyone when I do it. Walter says that we have to believe in it. We must believe in the Blue Light Energy. I trust Walter's word, so I trust in the Blue Light Energy, especially after seeing what Jules and Josh have done. These things were unheard of at home.

I stop a few yards away from the others. I close my fists, because for the first time, although I want to use my *field*, I do not want to feel it in my hands. This time, I feel it in my body. I feel the energy. I feel my *field*. I feel the shape and the muscle of it, and I feel its sensitivity to my surroundings. I want to replicate it.

With my fists at my sides, I relax and will myself—expect myself—to experience that same sensitivity in my surroundings using Blue Light Energy, and I begin to search for something in particular. As I expand the circumference of my search, I stumble upon three bodies a few yards behind me, emitting heat within three feet of each other, followed by empty space behind them. Then I feel it. Keeping my hands clenched, I grab the object in a *field* and believe in Blue Light for it to levitate off the floor. I spin around and find the pedestal and statue head on the right hovering above the floor, though nothing feeds through my hands to sustain it.

I am ecstatic and do not know what to say. I have never been able to sense things with my *field* without emitting it through my hands before. I have never been able to use my *field* at all without feeding it through my hands, let alone to lift things with it. I will have to develop this skill, starting with smaller objects, because using my *field* in this way takes time right now, but this is incredible.

Josh still looks stunned, and Jules looks like she might explode either in laughter or in a scream. Walter simply looks delighted at our excitement.

Josh is the first to try to speak. "Walter, this is ..."

"Impossible," Jules finishes.

Walter smiles. "Well, I am glad you think so."

I flex the *branches* in my wrists, realizing that I can probably do whatever I desire with them. Oddly enough, I believe that I can. I push just the tip of a *branch* out of my wrist and will there to be another right behind it. A second tip peeks out of my wrist, and a smile spreads across my face.

"Now, I understand that this is all very new and astounding for you three, but I am afraid that you are going to need to commence training for tonight."

I snap back into focus, quickly retracting my *branches*. I had forgotten about tonight in my momentary state of bliss.

"Of course," Josh says.

Josh and Jules are at attention again, and I walk back to rejoin them.

Walter acknowledges our eagerness with an appreciative nod and resumes. "Tonight is a relatively dangerous one, but Blue Light should be a very helpful tool. However, you must know how to use it. Unfortunately, it takes more training than we can afford to squeeze in before the expedition in order to really understand it and use it properly. However, based on your performance, I gather that you are very fast learners. We will see how much we can accomplish in this short period of time."

He walks to the mirror wall and faces us. "I want you to train, and train like your life depends on it. Whether we will face any form of danger tonight is unknown, but you need to be prepared for the worst-case scenario. When you tap into Blue Light, you have to be strong and confident. You also have to be strategic and know how you are going to use it. It serves as an advantage and an aid, but it will not do the work for you."

He pauses for a moment in contemplation. "We have a lot to do ... Josh, Jules, step to the side, please." He gestures to the wall that we entered the room through, and they move away from me. Simultaneously, Walter rapidly erects a multitude of four-foot pedestals around me with statue heads on them.

Surely, we are preparing for intense training. I do not know how it will be accomplished with a bunch of statue heads, but I have underestimated Walter and these heads before. I have no intention of doing so again. Without using my hands, I find my *field* within my center and will it to encompass me in a protective sphere for defense.

Walter strides purposefully to the side of the room, beside Josh and Jules.

"Begin!" he bellows, and the heads swivel in rapid, confusing movements as they circle me in different directions.

They swerve close to me and then away in random patterns,

and there is no way to track their movements except that they vaguely follow circular paths around my protective barrier. One pedestal *clones* itself into multiple copies, like the Killer I faced yesterday, only to retract into a single pedestal again. Another disappears and then reappears, *teleporting* throughout the space. Another zooms past me, holding a head with eyes that are turning red, likely to shoot a *laser* at me. Seemingly countless pedestals and heads swarm around me, traveling forward, then backward, to my left and then to my right, with untold *abilities*. It is chaos, but I can handle chaos.

I look for the head with the red eyes again, but before I find it, its *laser* finds my *field*. I grunt as the sudden powerful force thrusts me forward. It traces a ring of red around my *field* as it circles me, and I can feel it eating away at my protection like David's *ability*. The top of my protective sphere disappears at the line traced by the attack. I am running out of time.

I retract my sphere with the exception of one particular spot that I use as a shield and swivel around at the speed of the head to protect myself against its *laser beam*. Just as its eyes shift at the realization of the absence of my protective sphere, I lunge my *field* at it and immediately put my sphere back up, reverting my attention to the other heads as I hear the *laser* statue shatter to the floor.

Just as my defense system goes back up, numerous attacks suddenly bombard my *field*. It is hard to decipher where the onslaught comes from, because everything is happening so fast and constantly moving around me.

Then I realize the obvious course of action, but I cannot do it with a decomposing *field*. This sphere is being eaten away, so I will Blue Light to enable me to make another layer just outside this one and forcefully explode it outward, sending pedestals and heads crashing to the wooden floor. About ten pedestals reappear among the ruins, though. They must have disappeared just before being hit by my *field*. Evidently, simply knocking them over is not going to work.

More battering comes against my *field*. I lift the bottom of my sphere just enough to expel multiple *branches* from underneath it and circle them just outside the pedestals and their chaos. I do not know if they are intelligent enough to know what is behind them, but I am going to try. In an instant, I whip the moving heads with my *branches*, sending more heads toppling to the floor as I retract my *branches*, but two reappear together on my left and separate to continue circling me in opposite directions.

I take a chance with a confusing scenario. I drop my sphere of protection and will two planks of my *field* to appear—one in front of me and one behind me—in the paths of the circumventing heads as I dive into a roll diagonally to my right, dodging any attacks in my state of vulnerability. As I roll, I will those two planks to smash together in the direction of the two heads. I feel them make contact, and I rise from the roll to see the two statue heads clatter to the wooden floor.

Jules is next, and then Josh. We train like this for a while. How long it takes, I really do not know. People begin to descend the staircase during Jules's match, and the fascination in their eyes is apparent. They respectfully proceed through the doorway, but Walter eyes them to ensure that they do so.

After perhaps a half hour of further training, we are done, and Walter concludes it with a single statement: "It is time to go."

Chapter 13

WE COME THROUGH THE silver passageway and reach the hedge. It looks exactly the same in the late-evening light as it did last night and has an eerie familiarity. This is not a place that I particularly wanted to return to, but this is quite an exceptional case. Josh, Jules, and I are wearing the same black attire as everyone else on the mission.

Residual daylight still clings to the land in a blue haze, but it will dissipate to darkness very soon. Still, we are cautious for any sign of spies. Walter was clear that we are not to disturb them, though. The Firebursts are likely to know whenever one of their spies is attacked, and that would be just as danger-ous—if not more dangerous—as being reported by a spy. It is better to be reported by a spy in its own time as wanderers than for Firebursts to come out and meet us immediately, viewing us as an evident threat that is attacking their domain. Spies would not be able to report who we are, at least, because we are running with our black hoods draped over our faces. I can see why this is the ideal apparel for these operations.

Margaret, David, and John were glad to learn that we were coming on the operation. Margaret and David vowed to look out for us, though we insisted that it would not be necessary. John, on the other hand, simply snorted and said, "Well, at least you got enough training to do some real fighting around here." Delia was delightedly surprised, and her friends gave us a kind welcome.

Now here we are, crossing the place that joined us together. As I look up the grassy strip to my right, my mind flashes back to our rough encounter with the Resistance. Looking down the other way, I remember the spy that I saw last night.

We proceed to the hedge in silence, warned earlier by Walter not to make a sound. Our goal is to remain as invisible to the spies as possible. As we near the hedge, I consider opening a dome passageway through it with my *field*, but I do not want to leave anything disheveled or different in the hedge. Based on what I have heard, these spies are very meticulous. I consider *branching* over the hedge using the barren tree a few yards away again, but airborne projectiles may draw too much attention. We are only a few yards away from the hedge now, and I wonder what Walter has in mind to get to the other side. I watch him closely, looking for any sign of what we are to do.

Walter's fist comes up by his head, signaling us to halt. Before leaving for the expedition, Walter explained their key signals for silent communication to me, Josh, and Jules. This was one of them. Everyone freezes, and Walter appears to crumble into little pieces in the wind from head to toe. The same phenomenon happens to everyone else on the team in a ripple effect from the front of the group to those of us in the back. Panicked, I am wondering what is happening when I remember Walter's *ability*.

The ripple reaches me, and I close my eyes submissively as I lose focus of every molecule in my body and turn into vapor. Everything seems to be everywhere, and I lose touch with reality. There is nothing but nothingness.

Consciousness returns to me, and my thoughts find order as I realize that I am in one piece again. A couple of people *materialize* near me, but everyone ahead is already running again. I follow them, as do the people near me. I wonder who these people near me are and if I know any of them, but I do not bother to look, because I would not be able to see under their hoods. Our team is a simple mass of black, oblivious to our familiar groups or to our clusters of members from the same homeland. We are a single unit. Even Walter blends in with the rest of us, only set apart by his slight distance ahead.

We cross the lawn in front of the forsaken mansion, and memories briefly flash through my mind. I remember my glee and relief at the sight of Josh, saving Jules, recuperating in the golden evening light peering in through the window, the fear of new, imminent threats, and the narrow staircase spiraling out of the mansion. I notice the doorway that we left through as we jog by the side of the mansion.

The building looks the same as before, just like the hedge does. I did not expect them to look any different, but it is interesting to observe their consistency when our situation is so different from what it was yesterday. Noticing the line of trees bordering the mansion's lawn, I recall the first time that I saw Walter as he *materialized* out of thin air. Before, it was a fearful encounter. Now, we return only to blow in the wind with him.

Passing the mansion, I see that the lines of trees bordering it extend along a field that stretches to a curve in the distance to the left. Directly behind the mansion, a section of this expanse is fenced off to designate territory that belongs to the mansion. In the reserved land are a couple of trees: one in each far corner from the building, a few clusters of flowers scattered throughout the area, and a couple of white lawn chairs. Similar to the Resistance headquarters, the expanse here seems odd and misplaced.

Jogging into the open field, we do not have a lot of cover. We only have the few trees that randomly speck the field, and a strip about fifty yards ahead of us stretches out with almost no trees at all. We jog along the side of the field: near the trees, but we are out in the open nonetheless.

All is quiet except for our muffled steps as we jog through the grass. We are a dark pack of silence blending in with the looming night.

The jog would be relaxing if not for the vigilant search for spies or—even worse—Killers. Thankfully, there is no sign of either, but as we draw closer to the compound, I tense and find it more difficult to stay somewhat calm. I cannot find Jules among us, but I hope that she is all right coming back here. Out of the three of us, she had the roughest escape—the most dangerous.

We jog around the bend in the field and continue straight. The sky is just about black now, so everything has taken on the form of dark shadows. Nothing moves but for the dancing silhouettes of trees as they wave in the cool breeze. I still have not seen any sign of danger, which only makes me nervous, because we can only go so long before we run into trouble.

Far ahead is the silhouette of a very large building, but I cannot see it clearly from here. It sits at the foot of a hill in the middle of the field. We travel a considerable distance closer before I can see the compound better in the darkness as it rises into view over the edge of an apparent drop in our path. The building is wide and massive, and it resembles a cross between a mansion and a castle. It appears to be a light color in the shadows and comprises two tall stories, stretching maybe one hundred yards across. It is probably larger than the Resistance headquarters.

The scattered trees around us thicken into dense forests that border the plain by the time they reach the compound. On either side of the building, a narrow passageway of the field squeezes between the building and the forest, leading to the back.

As we jog closer to the descent in our path, more of the expanse comes into view. The bordering forest becomes more recessed, expanding the width of the open plain.

A tower protrudes from the left side of the compound, and a taller neighboring hill on the left fuses with the one behind the compound. A large bordering wall of rock extends as far as I can see along the other side of the massive hill. It must be a cliff of higher terrain, but I cannot tell in the darkness. I also cannot clearly see the indistinguishable peak of the towering hill standing proudly in the darkness. It practically invites some imminent threat to attack us. At any moment, a Killer—or perhaps a multitude of them—could appear from the other side of that hill and overtake us.

The forest climbs a portion of the tall hill, only to branch off into scattered trees. As we pass more trees bordering our path that hinder my view of the left side, a small clearing becomes visible by the rock wall in the midst of the forest. Squinting through the night, I see a waterfall there as well. Then I remember the waterfall that I saw when Josh and I *signaled* Jules yesterday and her description of her escape. That clearing is exactly where we found her. That is the hill where she fled for her life.

I remain vigilant for any sign of danger until Walter leads us into the forest on our right for concealment. As we enter, filing into a line by default, Walter's fist comes up only to open and slowly press down on the air, signaling for us to slow down. As we file through the forest and descend the slope in our path, we blend in with the dark shadows of the night, giving me a slight level of comfort. But we still need to be very careful of the sounds that we make as our feet shuffle among the countless dead leaves and fragile twigs on the ground.

Furthermore, though we may be difficult to notice, the inability to see around us in this forest slightly unnerves me, because there could easily be a spy here, concealed by the utter darkness. I try to look among the trees that tower over me for any sign of abnormal creatures or anything else out of the ordinary, but it is too dark to see anything. At least we should remain undetected.

We near the narrow strip of grass beside the compound. I can just barely see the people three feet in front of me—let alone Walter—but Walter must have raised his fist, because the people in front of me suddenly come to a halt. I follow their lead and stop right behind them. A few silent moments pass as I wait for the next move. Silent second after silent second extends into oblivion, and I grow anxious.

Suddenly, a bloodcurdling screech pierces the air from somewhere ahead. It is not deafeningly loud, but the sound and the pitch are enough to make my blood gurgle. I have never heard this shriek before, but I immediately know what it is: a Killer.

Everyone in front of me leaps into action, and I am right

behind them. I do not know exactly where the screech came from, or what has caused it, but I know that we are being successively led to wherever we need to go. I follow the train of shadows forward until we make a sharp turn out of the forest.

We are right beside the compound, and I wish that we were at least behind it, where there is open land and I would not feel so trapped if the shriek drew attention to us from the Firebursts.

In front of me, hooded shadows trace various *abilities* and *capabilities* all around two deeply red and marked faces in black suits: Killers. The hooded figures fight together to obliterate the two Killers, and it appears to be a breeze for them as one Killer collapses to the ground.

I fling my hand up, about to help my comrades and strike the other Killer down with my *field*, when something yanks me off my feet by my shoulders and into the forest. I stifle the urge to scream or yell, refusing to call anyone into danger and fearing that the sound will alert the Firebursts to our presence.

I land hard on my back several feet into the dark forest. Today's training has heightened my *field*'s sensitivity enough for me to sense something hovering over my head. I panic and lose control of my energy for an instant, emitting a gust of my *field* that pushes the attacker back. I use the advantage to scramble to my feet and swing around in a crouched position to face my unseen opponent, my *field* engulfing me in a standard bubble of defense.

I want to act immediately on the offensive. Thankfully, with Blue Light, I can attack from outside my bubble of defense without compromising my shield. However, I cannot see anything but utter darkness, and I do not want to attack blindly, provoking the Killer and their mysterious *abilities*, which may *deteriorate* my *field* of protection.

Suddenly, a ball of yellow-orange light flies past me into the darkness, and a muffled blue glow illuminates the night from behind me just as the airborne light hits a Killer. Another shriek makes my blood gurgle, and again I fear that it will draw the Firebursts to us.

The blue glow grows brighter in the darkness ahead of me as the light and its bearer come alongside me. The bearer's right hand is elevated by their head as they shine the blue light to chase away the darkness, and I am so grateful to them. They fling another ball of light ahead, revealing more Killers lurking among the trees just a few yards ahead of us. I cannot unequivocally distinguish how many there are, but I can see perhaps three curling their deep red faces into snarls.

A few other hooded silhouettes race into the battlefield as

the blue-light bearer provides a torch of light, and they all take action. No longer on the defensive, I drop my protection and move to join them, only to be intercepted by a Killer that suddenly appears right in front of me. My fist makes contact with the side of his face, reinforced by the power of my *field*. The Killer *teleports* out of my sight.

Just before I can engulf myself in a bubble of protection again, something stabs me in the side, causing a sharp pain. Still, I put up my defense and turn to the source of the attack, but all I see are tree silhouettes.

Suddenly, I sense something right behind me. I drop my defense to thrust my right elbow back with my *field* and as much physical strength as I can muster, hitting the Killer, and I follow through with a left hook that is just as strong. The Killer reels toward the edge of the forest, but I spew *branches* from my right hand to tie him up. I ensnare him from the neck down and emit a blow of force at him that I will—and believe—Blue Light to make my *branches* strong enough to withstand.

The Killer goes silent and still. I drop his body to the ground and turn to the rest of the battle.

Two Killers remain, fought off with various colors and movements from hooded figures masked in the dull light. The Killers' attention is not on me. I do not know if they even notice me, so I take advantage of the concealment. *Branches* run out of my wrists and race to the Killers' sides. I have to be careful, though, because I do not want to be hit by my own team in the crossfire. I whip the *branches* into the head of each Killer, disorienting them, and grab them with my *branches*, confining them from the arms down to keep them still while the hooded shadows bombard them to their defeat.

I raise the Killers above the ground, into the blue light, so that the team will clearly see my *branches* and be careful to avoid them. To be on the safe side, I will the Blue Light Energy within me to make my *branches* withstand any stray hits from my team or any purposeful attempts at liberation from my detainees.

There is intense writhing, but I believe in the Blue Light inside me to make me strong enough to withstand it. The bombardments from the shadow warriors draw earsplitting screeches from the Killers again, but I try to ignore them.

Never taking my eyes off the battle, I sensitize myself to my surroundings in case there are more surprises that may try to overpower me. I sense nothing, and no one in the battle hits my *branches*. When the squeals from the Killers and the assault from the silhouettes fall silent, I release the two bodies and retract my *branches*.

Despite the blue light faintly glowing in the Resistance member's hand, it is still dark here, and that makes me feel anxious. As a precautionary measure, I will and trust in Blue Light for my *field* to manifest in protective spheres around each of my teammates who return from the battle as well as around myself. As they retreat to the edge of the forest, I move with them, and we return to the narrow path beside the compound as one unit, where I release my protective spheres around everyone.

Two Killers lie on the ground in the path, eerily illuminated by the moonlight. I do not know if they are dead or unconscious, but for the team to have left them, I am sure that it must be safe.

I follow the team onto the path and toward the back of the compound. I only now notice that our team is divided when someone intercepts our path just before we turn the corner. A male voice discloses some piece of information to a couple of people ahead of me in hushed tones that I cannot decipher. The male turns around, and we follow him to the back of the compound.

Behind the building, the land stretches into the darkness until it reaches the peak of the hill and flows smoothly into the taller hill beside it. The taller hill towers over us, stretching into the dark sky that looms above. The moonlight gives a slight silver glow to everything and reflects off the compound in a vague radiance, contrasting with the horrors inside it.

Windows adorn the building, and a semicircular balcony extends from the upper floor, watching over the land. It stands upon ornate pillars that decorate complementary stairs to the back entrance. Ironically, the compound is a picture of beauty for something so wicked.

The rest of our comrades are jogging toward us from across the field. One of them reaches us just before the others. "We've located a few entrances," someone whispers. "The investigation is over. We need to get out of here while we still can."

Some of our group nod in silent agreement. We jog back to the narrow path from which we came, and I am unsure whether it is safer for us to go into the forest or to stay away from it in the open. Each option risks precarious scenarios.

More groups mysteriously rejoin us as we jog along the border of the forest. We avoid the noise of traveling through the leaves and twigs as we retreat from the compound. I just hope that no more Killers meet us. As a precaution, I stretch my *field* along the line of moving silhouettes in front of me and behind me. My hands are preoccupied as I run, so I emit the *field* by focusing on Blue Light, believing in it to emit the *field* from my body rather than specifically from my hands.

I sense my targets in my *field* as it stretches over them. Everyone is moving, though, so it takes concerted effort and focus to maintain protection for everyone. Nevertheless, I am determined to see this through. I left Josh and Jules vulnerable back at the hedge yesterday, and they were captured as a result of my carelessness. Thankfully, the Resistance was not there to harm us, but I do not wish to make that mistake again, especially under far more dangerous circumstances. This is my team. We are a unit. And I will do whatever I can to protect them.

We are still in view of the compound, but hopefully, we blend in with the night enough to mask our presence. As we ascend the slope in our path, my heart leaps in my chest when I notice a yellow bird fly by the forest on the other side of the field. The bird has a trailing, multicolored tail, for a purpose that I cannot even imagine. A yard ahead of it is a red bird that has an abnormally short body. Its wings are of a regular size, but its body looks about half the size of its wings. These birds are peculiar: spies. I tilt my head to ensure that my hood covers my face.

Up ahead, toward the peak of the ascent, scurrying across the field away from us, is a squirrel with something in its hands. I am suddenly so grateful for our tactical black attire and hope that no one's face is identifiable. We pass where I saw the scampering squirrel and leave the compound and all its dangers behind as we separate from the forest and jog through the field back to the Resistance headquarters.

Nothing pursues us, thankfully. I check throughout the entire trip back to headquarters. I just hope that the spies, seen or unseen, did not acquire enough information to endanger us.

Chapter 14

THE BRIGHT FOYER IN the mansion is tremendously welcome in my eyes. The huge chandelier, the large staircases, the promise of fortification and protection—even the infinite number of narrow claustrophobia-inspiring corridors—are more appreciated now than they were when we first arrived here. Initially, this place was a questionable institution of safety. Tonight, it is a trusted safe haven and a welcome fortress of security.

We all remove our bulky hoods, revealing our faces to one another. We were silent for the entire trip back. Now is the first time that we can really speak with one another and report our findings for the night.

"Is everyone here?" Walter asks from the front of the crowd.

"We made sure to stay in groups," a male up front says. "No one is reported to be absent."

I am still in the back, so I cannot see the person who spoke beyond the heads in front of me. I suppose his declaration explains how I was saved in the forest tonight. I never made a sound when I was yanked into the forest, yet covertly cloaked allies suddenly appeared to my rescue.

Thinking of the encounter, I become aware of a throbbing pain in my side. I look down to see a rip in my clothes and a wound peeking out underneath that slickens the edges of the material with blood. I do not examine it any further, because I do not want to psychologically feed the pain that I already feel.

"Very good." Walter nods, glancing over the crowd, verifying everyone's presence. With a satisfied look, he says, "We will continue this in the lounge."

He walks to the lounge area, and we all follow him into the comforting, lush space. Everyone disperses. Some go to scattered lounge chairs, others stand by the windows, and some race to the couch and chairs that surround the little wooden table.

I head in the direction of the couch, when two unfamiliar faces take a seat on it, shortly joined by Margaret, David, and Josh, who sit on the couch and in its neighboring chairs. Jules approaches and sits on the arm of the nearest chair, but Josh insists that she sits in the seat of the furniture while he sits on the arm. Seeing that the area is full, I change course to go stand beside a window.

"Sophie!"

I look back at David.

"Here," he says, and he stands up.

I try to decline the offer, but he insists. So, I come back and sit on the couch while he sits on the arm next to me. Margaret, who sits in the farther chair, wears an intense look on her face—the look of a warrior—and I know that her mind is elsewhere.

"What we have accomplished this evening is greater than we could have hoped for," Walter says, coming to the front of the room on the rug pathway. "Though we came across a number of difficulties, we have discovered significant passageways and details to improve our approach to storm the compound. Thanks to the input of Josh and a few other contributors, we have a greater level of understanding regarding our enemies. Half of the battle is knowing our opponent, and tonight we have gained substantial knowledge of the compound, which we will recap tomorrow when it is not so late in the day."

I wonder what exactly was discovered about the compound

for Walter to feel so accomplished.

"Now, as for the Killers, I may have a fairly accurate hypothesis as to their purpose there at the compound. The Firebursts are a widespread, destructive organization. They are not confined to any single region. They travel far and wide, wreaking havoc on whoever and whatever they put their hands on. However, they need a sort of guard system now to keep things in order."

Walter pauses to look at Josh, Jules, and me. "If the Killers were there only for you, it would serve no purpose for them to stay there. Even if they did not know that you had successfully escaped from the compound, they would have tried to break in and come after you. Whether they succeeded or failed at targeting you there, they would have left by now."

I cannot help but feel slightly delighted at the good news. It would seem that there are no additional, unknown pursuers coming after us.

Walter looks back up at the rest of the group in the lounge area. "The Killers serve as a top-notch security system. No one can get in or out without getting by them. No one can approach the compound without facing them—"

"I thought that the spies served as their security system," Jules interrupts.

"They do, but they are only a precautionary measure. They have been their security system for quite some time now and are meant to spot slight disturbances. No one has ever really approached the compound before, to the Firebursts' knowledge. Now, however, they expect opposition. They know that a resistance is developing and opposition is to be expected. Any attempt from it or any other organization is to be utterly obliterated at the sign of approach." Seemingly to himself, he quietly adds, "Just as they obliterate everything else."

My focus sways as the pain from the wound intensifies, seeming to reach across and claw at my insides. It is a strange, uncomfortable pain that is very distracting. I have never felt anything like this before.

Walter continues. "This will intensify our operations, and we need to make sure that we are properly trained and ready. Appropriate measures need to be taken to ensure adequate preparation. The number of Killers that we faced tonight could have been a small fraction of the total number of Killers on-site. I do not know how many are scattered about the compound, nor do I know their distribution about the structure. However, rest assured there are more. The Firebursts are relentless and logical. To only distribute a few Killers about the compound's perimeter would be illogical."

His face contorts into a frown of deep thought, and he looks as if he is on the verge of pacing. "There could be various reasons behind only having a select few on patrol tonight. Perhaps they were only intended to strike fear into the hearts of adversaries, or to test enemies and see how proficient they are. We cannot be sure, but we need to be ready in case there are many more." He clasps his hands behind his back, and he stands at ease, observing us. "Dismissed."

A wave of bodies simultaneously initiates movement and walks to the archway leading to the foyer. I need to have this wound on my side tended to, but I decide to let everyone exit before I cross the room to go to Walter.

Josh and Jules look back and notice that I am still on the couch. Everyone has left, so I move to stand up. My efforts are thwarted, however, when a sharp pain shoots up my side and across my abdomen—worse than the cuts, burns, and bruises from the compound, which I have come to barely even notice.

The crippling pain threatens to knock me down. But I push past it, stand up, and walk over to Walter, holding my wet side with my hand and ignoring the concerned looks that Josh and Jules send my way.

"Walter ..." Oddly enough, I sound out of breath, and it takes me aback. *What is wrong with me?* "I need to go to the medical wing."

Walter's eyes trail down to my hand on my side. He gently takes my hand and removes it slightly. Refusing to look at the wound, I watch his eyes widen, and he replaces my hand. With one hand on my arm and the other on my back, he swiftly escorts me toward the exit.

"This way," he urges.

We pass Josh and Jules.

"What is wrong with her?" Josh asks as he and Jules walk with us. His voice sounds a little groggy, though, and I do not understand why.

"She has been poisoned."

"What? How?" interjects Jules.

Everyone sounds muffled, and my vision suddenly becomes blurry.

"A Killer," Walter responds gravely.

Fear whips through me like a tidal wave. *Poisoned ... by a Killer ...* The despair in Walter's voice sinks in as I realize this is a death sentence. *My* death sentence.

Something overtakes me, stripping me of the strength to stay on my feet, and I'm suddenly drowned in darkness.

Author's Note

Thank you so much for reading *More Than Conquerors: On the Run*. I hope you enjoyed this debut novel in the series. Ever since I started writing this on a few loose-leaf pages in 2012, I've been eager to share this story with others. I enjoyed the suspense, the bravery, and the tragedy (I'm a big high stakes fan), but there was something more to this story for me. It's the hope behind it, the symbolism behind Blue Light Energy, the strength in unity and in holding one another up when you just can't stand up on your own anymore—it's the depth and the meaning behind this story that really gets me and that makes it the dearest and closest one to my heart (so far).

I can't share all of it in just these few sentences here, but you can scan the QR code on the next page or visit the website link to learn more about this story and its meaning. And there are other surprises there, too, for those who just want something fun and entertaining.

This has been a long journey to get this published, and there have been multiple hurdles. But, sometimes, obstacles come with the territory of producing something special. And I hope this story and the messages behind it will be a special light in your life as it has been in mine.

"Two people are better off than one, for they can help each other succeed. If one person falls, the other can reach out and help..."
– Ecc. 4:9-10
"And be sure of this: I am with you always, even to the end of the age." – Matt. 28:20b
"...And He will give you another Helper ... to be with you forever." – John 14:16

P.S. I am truly so grateful to my mother and to my dearest friend who have both believed in me to publish my stories and encouraged me to stay true to the gifts God has given me.

Take an Adventure Deeper Into
MTC: On the Run

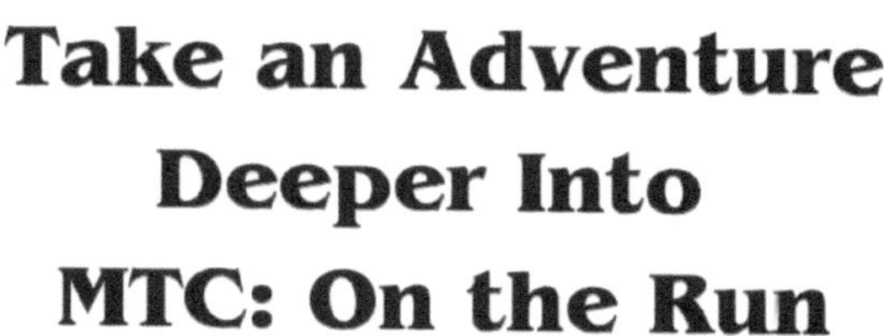

www.djaneecreations.com/newsletters

The story, characters, and
surprises as bright as
Blue Light Energy

A fan of YA Dystopian Books?

Find The Blizzard's Secrets on Amazon

About the Author

D JANÉE IS BOTH AN author and a poet. As an author, she writes material ranging from children's books to young adult fiction. As a poet, she writes inspirational poetry highlighting the beauty in everyday life.

In books such as *The Blizzard's Secrets, Jimmy and the Teddy Bear* and *More Than Conquerors: On the Run*, she highlights wholesome principles and exciting adventures to captivate, inspire, and encourage young readers. When she is not writing poetry or stories, she is learning something new, such as a new language or a new skill. She also loves traveling with loved ones.

You can visit her website at www.djaneecreations.com.

Facebook, Instagram, Pinterest: @djaneecreations.